Second Chances for Trampled Hearts

Sweet inspirational
contemporary cowboy romance

Book 1 in

the Bear Creek Saddle Series

by *NY Times* & *USA Today* bestselling author
Shoshanna Evers
writing as

Shoshanna Gabriel

Second Chances for Trampled Hearts

Stand-alone first book in the Bear Creek Saddle Series by Shoshanna Evers writing as Shoshanna Gabriel

A handsome rancher who lost his faith along with his young wife.

A waitress, abandoned by her cheating ex, and looking for a fresh start...

Allie Crawford buys half-ownership of the cowboy's diner in the small mountain town of Bear Creek Saddle, Idaho. It's all she can afford, and it's about as far from Miami as she can get. Will it be far enough?

"Big Bad Bill" inherited the town's infamous old diner from his great-uncle, who insisted it stay in the family. Bill knows cattle, not the restaurant business—so he'll foot the bill to get it going again, and let the woman chomping at the bit for her own restaurant handle running it.

Then Allie needs his help with renovations, and Bill finds he can't stay away, after all.

Neither expects the friendship that blooms between them. But even beautiful evergreen trees and soaring mountain peaks can't soothe the pain of betrayal and loss.

Faith may be the only thing big enough to heal their trampled hearts, and give them both a second chance at love...

Second Chances for Trampled Hearts is *NY Times* and *USA Today* bestselling author Shoshanna Evers' first inspirational romance writing as Shoshanna Gabriel.

Keep reading for **BONUS CONTENT** after "The End" — read the first chapter of *Bear Creek Saddle Cowboy*, Book 2 in the series!

Second Chances for Trampled Hearts
Book 1 in the Bear Creek Saddle Series
by Shoshanna Gabriel

Note: A different version of "Second Chances for Trampled Hearts" was originally released in 2015 as "I Am Not Your Melody" by the same author writing as Shoshanna Evers

Author's Note to the Reader

The story behind the story...and what happened when I came out as a Christian.

YOU MAY KNOW ME as Shoshanna Evers, a *New York Times* and *USA Today* bestselling author of steamy romance. Maybe you have even read the book that this one is based on: *I Am Not Your Melody*, which was part of the Cowboy 12-Pack—a digital book bundle that hit the *New York Times* and *USA Today* bestseller lists in 2015. So why the big changes? And what *are* the changes?

Quick background on why I've had to change everything—my career, my religion, and my name. It's the beginning of 2016 as I write this (and a year later, April 2017, as I finish). About two years before I started this book, I had a "road to Damascus" experience, and I started to think about Jesus as the Messiah. I'm Jewish, so that was something I had literally never thought about before. At that point in 2014, I had gone from writing erotic romance to less-explicit but still very steamy romance, (books that came out that year had been written the year before). In 2015 when I bit the bullet and got baptized (despite the extreme disapproval of my secular Jewish family), things started changing for me very fast, from the moment I came out of the water.

I had been getting more and more successful as Shoshanna Evers. Writing sexy stories was very good to me, but it wasn't good *for* me, personally—not when it was keeping me from writing the stories I truly wanted to tell. I found myself writing faith elements into my storylines, only to have to remove them because they weren't part of the Evers "brand". I didn't want to freak out my readership, who hadn't signed on for anything having to do with God. Most importantly, I started feeling weird about what I was doing with my writing. I wanted to use the gift He had given me in a way that would be for His glory.

I'd never felt ashamed or weird about writing sexually explicit stories before—and to this day I won't judge those who do. But something had changed in me. Writing love scenes was no longer my thing, which—considering I had written and had been editor of the non-fiction book *"How to Write Hot Sex"* in 2011—was going to mean *a major overhaul* in my life.

When I wrote *I Am Not Your Melody*, which I called "a Bear Creek Saddle short novel" and prequel to an upcoming series, I was already tired of writing sex scenes (after writing them in every book since 2010, I had essentially burned myself out). And my hero, Bill, was clearly (to me) having a faith crisis, but I couldn't articulate that. When the book came out, it wasn't the book I had really wanted to write in the first place. Despite that, I knew the book was good and that it fulfilled the promise I'd made to my readers as Shoshanna Evers: *Sexily *Evers* After*. It sold fifteen thousand copies in the first week as part of the Cowboy 12-Pack, and kept on selling.

The follow-up series was bought by a big publisher. My literary agent and I were going back and forth with them on the book delivery dates, because during the negotiations my husband and I found out, first, that we were expecting a baby (yay!) and then a few weeks later, that we were actually expecting twins (gasp! And YAY!!). I knew I'd have my hands full even without worrying about book deadlines. Now I think God was keeping me from signing on the dotted line, to give me more time to reevaluate my career.

I realized I couldn't sign the contract. I was just…*done* writing secular romance. There was no way I'd be able to write the series the way the publisher wanted me to. Instead, I wanted to write inspirational romance. They were very gracious and let me out of the contract. My agent—who was also very gracious—and I parted ways because she didn't represent Christian fiction. In one fell swoop I had lost a six-book contract and my agent, and though it felt as if I were pressing the career-self-destruct-button, I wrote a blog post entitled "Saying Goodbye to Erotic Romance" (http://bit.ly/GoodbyeErotica) in November 2015, where I came out as a Christian, and told my readership what was happening.

The response was overwhelmingly wonderful. My loyal readers assured me they loved the way I tell stories, so they'd still read my books, and the Christian romance author community was so kind and welcoming. For some reason, I'd expected them to keep their distance, since I was "that kind" of author who had written "those kind" of books, and I didn't belong over in the squeaky-clean section of the cafeteria. But just the opposite happened—the inspirational authors welcomed me with open arms. Those ladies really walk the talk, friends.

There have been, of course, some readers who are upset. They've told me they're done reading my books. The day after the blog post went out, I had to step down as the Erotica Captain for a big annual book convention. I had created panels and topics, and I was going to be speaking on them as well. The panels went forward, but without me on them. The decision hurt my pride a bit, but it made sense. I needed a clean break in order to move forward.

Shoshanna Gabriel is my new name for my new genre. No more *Sexily *Evers* After*, now my promise is a *Faithfully Ever After*. Originally, I wanted to keep the name Shoshanna Evers, since I've spent nearly 6 years building it up and had my "letters" (*NYT & USAT*)—but I have too many sexy books out as Evers, and I didn't want my future readers to accidentally pick up a backlist book and have a heart attack. Giving up my bestseller status to start all over again wasn't an easy decision, but it's one I made after a lot of prayer, and it feels right.

Thanks for reading this, and for giving *Second Chances for Trampled Hearts*—my first inspirational romance—a try. If you had previously read the steamy version, you'll notice the bar has become a diner, and the sex scene and cussing are gone. Turns out, they weren't needed anyway. Mostly, the vibe is sweeter and with a Christian outlook. God's love is front and center instead of sexual attraction. And hey, I have good news—the Bear Creek Saddle series is still happening! I've gotten a new agent who represents Christian fiction, and—for this particular series—I am indie-publishing to get the books to you more quickly. This book is a full story and completely stand-alone, with no cliffhangers.

So hold onto your cowboy hats, and happy reading! Please pray for me, friends, and I'll be praying for you.

All my best wishes,

Shoshanna Gabriel

April 2nd, 2016 - June 24th, 2017

Chapter One

"For I know the plans I have for you," declares the Lord, "plans to prosper you and not to harm you, plans to give you hope and a future." ~Jeremiah 29:11 (NIV)

THE LOW GAS LIGHT on Allie Crawford's dash had been flashing for the last fifteen miles. She'd make it to Melody Ranch though, she had to. There was no more money in her bank account or cash in her wallet to fill up, in any case. But she'd never get there if she kept driving around in circles.

Cold wind found its way into the car's back passenger-seat window, since it wouldn't close that last eighth of an inch. And this wasn't Miami-cold, aka sixty degrees Fahrenheit. No. It was only November and yet up here in the mountains of north Idaho, it may as well have been winter.

Then again, Allie had no clue what a real mountain winter was like, so, maybe this was normal "fall" weather here in Bear Creek Saddle?

She exhaled heavily. Was she even going the right way? The small town—well, small in number (648 residents, according to the

Welcome sign) but huge if you took into account the sprawling acreage—was laid out in a way no developer ever would have planned. Large mountains, evergreen trees, lakes, and creeks interrupted the land, and the roads followed the landscape—no matter how twisty and turny things got. Allie couldn't even imagine having to traverse the roads when they were covered in ice and snow.

"I'm a reverse snowbird," she murmured.

Everyone else goes south for winter, and Allie goes north. Of course.

Melody Ranch wasn't easy to find, despite her GPS's best efforts. It was as if the road to the ranch didn't really exist. She'd need to get directions from a local.

A sign that read "Ginger's General Store" caught her eye. Allie pulled over on the main street in town, sighing with relief when she got out of the car. Finally, a chance to stretch her legs.

She smoothed her clothes, rumpled from the seatbelt. At the Washington/Idaho border, she'd stopped at a rest stop and changed out of her comfy jeans and T-shirt into her emerald-green blouse, black pants, and heels from Payless that looked more expensive than they'd cost (to her eyes, at least).

This was her new life in a new town, and Allie intended on dressing the part of "successful business owner" starting with her very first face-to-face meeting with Bill Edwards. Which—if she managed to actually locate him—would be shortly.

But really, after the several months of email interaction they'd had, the cattle rancher who'd sold her a fifty-percent share of his late uncle's diner business (along with the apartment above the diner) wasn't a stranger. Despite Bill Edwards' no-nonsense emails at first, it hadn't taken long for his personality and glimpses of life on Melody Ranch to shine through in his writing.

She liked to read his emails to herself in his accent, which she'd heard in one brief phone call early on. "Wait'll you see the stars up here on a clear night, Allie… in the summer the guys an' I camp out jus' to see 'em. Yeah, city-girl, I'll teach ya to build a campfire they ain't never seen in Miami… You're gonna love it here."

Now, though they'd never met—and she'd never even seen a photo of him for goodness sake, despite some late-night Googling—Allie knew *him*. He'd told her too much for him to be a stranger when they would finally get to meet in person. They already got along so well (online, at least). Maybe when they met, she'd skip the handshake and go straight to a hug?

There was something that attracted her to Bill. Nothing overt…maybe it was just his masculinity. His personality came through his emails. If Paul Bunyan had written emails during his lumberjacking adventures, she imagined he'd have sounded a lot like Bill Edwards did when he wrote to her.

Allie shook her head. It was silly to have feelings for a man she'd never met. He might not even be too happy to see her, actually. Bill didn't strike her as the type of guy to appreciate surprises.

If she had contacted Bill to tell him she'd be showing up earlier than they'd agreed on, then he could have said no. And if he'd said no, she'd be in hot water. Her money was tied up in the diner and her new home above it, yet rent was due in Miami. She needed that apartment *now*, not in two weeks.

Better to ask for forgiveness than ask for permission, right? That's exactly what she'd do when the man from the emails would finally stand before her.

As soon as she figured out how to find him.

A bell rang to announce Allie's presence when she pulled open the door to the general store. The place was a huge departure from the franchised, big-box stores she always shopped in, in Miami. Wooden tables were set up around the open space, each covered with a selection of goods. On one table, crates of fresh produce with "local" scrawled on a black chalkboard sign. On another table, piles of used paperbacks, fifty cents apiece. *Books!* And there was jam, lined up in beautiful glass jars, hand-labeled with an artisan touch. Then there were the… fish hooks. And buckets of hard wheat.…

General, indeed.

"Good morning," the middle-aged woman behind the register counter called. "We just got in more huckleberry jam, if that's what you're lookin' for!"

"Um…" Allie looked from the table of jam to the woman. It hadn't occurred to her to look for huckleberry jam, but now that the woman mentioned, it did look good.

No money. Right.

"Haven't seen you before," the woman said, stepping out from behind the counter. Her T-shirt proclaimed I MAKE QUILTS. WHAT'S YOUR SUPERPOWER?

"I'm moving here, actually." Allie smiled.

Bill had already warned her that news spread fast in a small town, and so her first impression on folks was even more important here than it would be if she were moving to a big city, where she could've counted on being relatively anonymous. Like that country song said, "Everybody Dies Famous in a Small Town."

"Oh, how wonderful!" the woman effused, her round face expressing a mix of surprise and interest. "No one ever moves here, pretty much ever. I'm Ginger by the way, it's on the sign."

"Allie Crawford." She tamped down her exhaustion from the road trip, and frustration with trying to find the ranch, so that she could smile warmly as she shook Ginger's hand.

"What can I do for ya?" Ginger asked. She'd said it in the sort of way a person asks when they actually want to know, rather than out of courtesy. "I saw you eyein' the fishing hooks. We got fishing licenses here too, if ya need one."

Allie laughed—she wouldn't know how to fish if her life depended on it—but the offer hadn't been a joke, so she stopped and just shook her head.

"I just can't seem to find Melody Ranch," she sighed, some of her earlier frustration creeping back into her voice. "I'm looking for Mr. Bill Edwards?"

Ginger raised her eyebrows, and meandered over to the big front windows of the store, where she peered out to stare at Allie's car.

"Florida plates," she mused. "Long way to go to find Big Bad Bill."

Big Bad Bill? Was she talking about the same Bill?

"Um…yes," Allie said. "He's expecting me."

That wasn't exactly false. He was expecting her two weeks from now. But when the first of the month came, she would've either had to pay another month of rent or leave her Miami apartment. The long road trip cross-country from Florida to north Idaho was the best option.

She'd wait for the grand tour—and the keys—until Bill could show her the diner they now shared. Back in Miami, she'd thought she would be too excited to do anything else when she got here. That she'd roll into town, pull right up in front of "her" diner, and… what? Mark her territory? Plant a flag like she was on the moon?

Instead, Allie was content to find Bill first thing—her one and only contact in the whole state of Idaho.

Maybe her avoidance was a little bit because she was terrified. She might take one look at the building and business she'd bought a fifty percent share of sight unseen—relying only on emails and photos from a man who technically, really was a complete stranger—and start freaking out.

What if she'd made a huge mistake?

Ginger shrugged her shoulders. "You prob'ly want to see Zach, or Eric. Or you know, Chris or Jay. Any of them can help you—the boys practically run the place now."

"The boys... Bill has children?" Allie asked. *He never told me that.*

The woman laughed uproariously. "Could you imagine? Oh, you are a firecracker!" She paused to wipe her eyes, which had teared up at the apparent hilarity of Allie's question.

"I take it Bill Edwards isn't the children...type?" While Allie and Bill had never found a reason to speak about kids, it was surprising to hear that about him.

Maybe Allie and Ginger were talking about two different Bill Edwards at Melody Ranch.

Okay, not likely.

"No," Ginger said, "I guess they ain't really boys no-more—his ranch hands. Time flies, don't it? Seems like yesterday they were runnin' in here for pop after school, on their way to the ranch to work... but I guess that was oh, ten years ago?"

Ginger groaned, as if suddenly realizing a decade had passed without her noticing. "I tell ya, time flies, it just flies. Can't even call 'em boys any more. *Handsome* young men, all four of them. Smart, too. It's no wonder Big Bad Bill let them take over everything!"

Allie smiled, still unsure of what was going on. The whole *Big Bad Bill* thing was disconcerting, as if she were about to encounter a villainous wolf.

"You married?" Ginger asked, a glint in her eye.

Allie grit her teeth. Of course, Ginger had no idea that was an extremely sore subject. Wasn't Ginger's fault. But if Allie told the woman her former husband of ten short months had run away with his secretary, it would be all over town by nightfall.

The judge had annulled their marriage, as if it had never happened at all. She didn't have to consider herself a divorcée. That ugly skeleton could stay firmly in the closet, *thankyouverymuch*. In Bear Creek Saddle, only Bill knew her past.

"Nope," Allie said, in response to Ginger's question. "Not married."

"The boys at Melody Ranch are single too, ya know," Ginger said.

Quite the matchmaker, very subtle.

It was flattering actually, considering Ginger couldn't really know if Allie was a good match, and yet the woman was already trying to pair her up with a cowboy from the ranch. Allie's choice out of four, no less. That could be awesome… but she'd already decided that staying away from men was probably the safest way to avoid having her heart torn in two again.

Her ex's betrayal still stung, even a year later. More than stung.

"Maybe the boys *could* help me," Allie said, trying to turn the conversation away from dating and back around to getting directions. "But… Bill Edwards *is* at Melody Ranch, right? I can find him there?"

The woman leaned in close, as if she were about to tell a secret. Allie looked around. There was literally no one else in the shop.

Still, Ginger dropped her voice. "I don't know what business you've got with Bill that ya can't take care of with the boys, but I wish you luck, that's all I'm sayin'. You seem like a sweet girl. Keep your chin up, and don't let him scare you."

"*Scare* me?" Allie swallowed hard. Maybe she'd been duped. Catfished. "Ginger, is he… dangerous?"

This time, the woman did not laugh. "No. Not dangerous. Just mean." She stopped abruptly, and took a breath, her demeanor back to friendly-shop-owner mode. "No one blames Bill, though, bless him. A man shouldn't have to lose his wife so young."

Hmm.

Ginger shook her head as if to clear her thoughts. "Well, anyway that's just my opinion. Just trying to help you out; I'm not one to gossip—"

Allie couldn't even smile at that. She was still trying to absorb all the new information that had been thrown at her. Bill had been married…his wife had passed away. All pieces of the puzzle that made up her new business partner.

"Honey," Ginger said sincerely, "if you get yourself into any trouble with Big Bad Bill, I betcha one of the boys on the ranch will come to the rescue." She smiled.

"Why do you keep calling him that?" Allie asked.

Please don't be because he's a criminal or con artist.

"Oh, just a silly nickname," Ginger said, waving her hand as if to brush the connotation of the nickname off. "Ya know, 'cause Bill Edwards is the biggest, baddest cowboy in town. We know it, he knows it, and I guess pretty soon you will too!" This time, her laughter kicked up, softening the words.

Ginger pointed out the big window. "Look, honey—Allie, right? —you just need to take Pleasantview all the way 'round till ya hit the foot of the mountain. Drive past the train tracks and make a right. You'll start seein' signs, and smell the cows."

Allie repeated the directions back to the woman, grateful to finally know where she was going. "Thank you for…all of that information." She backed out of the shop quickly, before she could get caught up in another long conversation.

Ginger called to her as Allie was already climbing back into her car. "Whatcha need to see Bill about, anyways?"

After everything the woman had told her about "Big Bad Bill," Allie didn't doubt that anything she'd told the woman would never stay quiet. She pretended not to hear the question.

"Thanks!" Allie called back over her shoulder. "See you next time!"

* * *

A half hour later, Allie pulled up to a large log entrance-way that declared she had finally found her destination. The ranch was huge, and she couldn't possibly be seeing all of it. Cattle grazed peacefully—despite the cold weather that morning—on either side of her car, on fields that went on forever. Only the farm buildings and the mountains broke up the skyline. An old ranch farmhouse loomed on the left. Mud-splattered pickup trucks were parked in the gravel lot outside of it.

It was beautiful land…the sort of thing she'd only seen before in movies that were set out West. If she didn't adapt quickly, the culture shock from all the differences between north Idaho and Miami could be all-consuming.

She parked next to a beat-up red pickup truck and released her seatbelt. Okay. This was happening…finally. That was a good thing, so why was she so fearful?

Reality hit her like a splash of cold water. A lot hinged on this meeting.

Bill had only sold her half of his diner because he needed

somebody to handle everything—the whole project of renovating the diner, opening it up, and running the business. What if he took one look at her, and thought she was nothing like her emails? He might think Allie was all talk, but not up to the task.

Stop projecting. Those were her own concerns, not Bill's.

Admittedly, she'd never owned a business before, but she'd been a waitress for years, and a good one. For the last two years, she'd even been promoted to shift manager, which gave her a better view behind-the scenes of the restaurant. She'd also taken an online course in business management to try and get up to speed on the nitty-gritty aspects. Yes, it was a short course, but Allie studied the material as carefully as she would've at a real college.

That had to count for something. That, and her motivation to prove to herself that she *could* do it, that she was absolutely capable of owning a business and running it well. Forget her cheating ex, forget her anonymous life in Miami, living paycheck to paycheck. The clean mountain air here, the small town, the beauty of it all…she was home now, in Bear Creek Saddle, and ready to start over. She could feel it in her soul.

A quick glance in the rearview mirror confirmed her blonde hair looked like she'd combed it with the wind. She found her purple mini-brush at the bottom of her purse and swiped it through her hair.

What if the things she wanted to do to restore the diner ended up costing too much for Bill? As part of their deal, he'd promised he would fund all improvements of the diner upfront (and get paid back with an extra percentage of the profit until they were even, at which point they'd split profits 50-50). She wanted to put a space for live music in… but he hadn't sounded too excited about that in his emails. Would he simply close the purse strings? There was no way she could pay the tens of thousands of dollars it was going to take to make this diner a success without him.

Allie stepped out of the car, smoothed her blouse once more, and looked around for someone to point her in the right direction. The wind was picking up, blasting cold air right through the thin material.

The car door handle was freezing when she opened the car again to grab her jacket—a thick, beige wool pea-coat she'd always thought made her look a bit like Eponine from the musical *Les Misérables* (one of her favorite musicals ever, definitely). And like Eponine, she was on her own and broke, so the coat fit her dire situation.

"Hello?" Allie called, buttoning up. No one responded.

In fact, no one seemed to be around at all. Only the cattle. Down the dirt road a bit there were some stables. Maybe Bill was tending to his horse. He'd already told her he was in the process of taming a wild stallion that had needed medical help for a wound.

It was weird to be there, knowing details about the ranch from Bill's emails without ever having been there before.

Allie pulled out her phone to text him. May as well give him a heads-up that she was there...even if he'd be upset. Her fingers clasped around nothing but air in her pocket.

You have got to be kidding me. Now she'd have to ransack the car, then retrace her tracks all the way back to Ginger. Thank goodness she had her missing phone password-protected, in case Ginger wanted to go through it (searching for a way to help Allie get her phone back, of course. Nothing to do with gossip.)

But now that Allie had finally gotten to the ranch, after almost a week on the road...the last thing she wanted to do was jump back in the car and leave. Later, yes. Now: find Bill.

Allie walked on the dirt path down to the barn. Somebody would probably be there, at least.

"Hello?" she called again.

A horse in the stables whinnied in response, and Allie grinned.

"Yay!" She whispered her cheer, just for herself. It had been quite a while since she'd last gotten an opportunity to say hi to horses.

They were such amazing animals. When she was a kid, she had taken home a blue ribbon in Dressage. But her equestrian hobby was too expensive to keep up after her mom divorced, and so she'd had to say goodbye to her horse Salsa and her riding lessons, right at the same time her dad moved out.

Uh oh… did that sound like stomping hooves?

This horse did not look happy. The closer she got to the stable, the huger the horse appeared, practically filling the stall with his muscular body. He flattened his ears when he saw her approach and shook his head.

"Are you the wild one?" she whispered.

She didn't see the wound Bill had told her about from her vantage point, but this didn't look like a domesticated working horse—not at all. It had to be the one Bill was trying to tame.

The fact that Bill had emailed to tell her about it the moment he got a chance after rescuing the injured animal made her giddy in a silly, girly way—because that meant Bill saw her as a friend, the way she'd begun to see him.

It was the ride of my life, Allie, he'd written to her, *I wish you were here already to see how strong and…beautiful…this stallion is. Takes my breath away.*

He'd been right—the stallion was beautiful. But its strength made it dangerous.

"Whoa… it's okay. Look," she said, keeping her hands at her sides. "I'm taking a step back, no worries."

The stallion still looked like he wanted to kill her. She turned and walked several feet more away. Maybe that would calm it down, make it stop moving in that angry, restless way.

Something was wrong with that horse. Maybe the horse was acting that way because he'd injured himself banging around in the stall like that. Or maybe his wound was really hurting him, or infected or something.

"Is anybody here?" she called, walking across in front of the stable to see if someone was working on the other side of the structure.

The stallion neighed in fright, and rushed forward, shaking the wooden stall door.

Allie looked up at the horse, willing the wave of fear that flowed through her not to show in her body language. She'd never dealt with a wild horse before. Her attempts at calming it would've worked on a show horse, maybe, but not this guy.

Maybe what she'd thought was giving him enough space wasn't enough at all.

The stallion stomped his foot, quivers of tension rippling across his back.

I'm too close for him. "Whoa!"

With a lunge, the horse popped the latch on the gate, pushing the wood down to the ground with a mighty crash.

Allie shrieked, and leapt to the side to get out of the way. She fell backward over her heels, landing in the dirt with her legs sprawled, and the horse dangerously close.

Suddenly the sound of hooves rushed up behind her, and for a terrifying split-second, she thought she was about to be trampled to death.

Please God, NO!

Her body lurched into the air, her arms in a painful, unknown vise.

"Help!" she screamed.

She wasn't sure if she was yelling for help from the wild stallion, or for help from the huge, mean-looking cowboy who had just lifted her up and thrown her across his saddle in front of him.

Chapter Two

THE MAN ON THE horse held her still, keeping her immobilized. One heavy, muscular arm lay across her lower back, as if he were prepared to spank her.

"What did you do to that horse?" the man yelled. His icy gray eyes flashed with anger, and it was all directed at her.

"That horse almost killed me!"

The stallion had taken off, galloping around through the nearest pasture, which was thankfully empty of cattle. At least the fences should keep him away from her.

Her elbows and her bottom hurt from her fall, but her pride hurt much worse at being manhandled and thrown over the back of a horse by this man.

A *handsome* man, at least beneath the scruff and anger on his face. He must be one of the ranch hand "boys" Ginger had basically suggested Allie marry.

The cowboy grabbed her under the armpits and roughly pulled her to sitting, without bothering to tell her he was going to do so first. She winced as her seat hit the saddle.

"Get your grubby hands off of me."

The cowboy raised his hand and she flinched. No, he wasn't going to hit her.

He looked at his hand, checking out the lines of dirt under his fingernails. "Did I ruin your *wardrobe*?" he asked, dripping sarcasm. "Gettin' trampled by that wild stallion would've mussed you up even worse."

"I knew it!" she said. "I knew he was wild. You guys shouldn't keep him locked up like that. He hates it."

"That ain't your business," he snapped.

Without warning, he wrapped his thick, muscular arm around her waist to keep her from falling off, and squeezed his thighs against his horse's flanks to make it move. The familiar feel of a horse trotting beneath her, merged with the altogether unfamiliar feel of a large muscular man holding her pressed against him.

"I'm takin' you back to wherever you came from," he said, "and then I gotta undo what you just did—messin' up Pirate's training."

Allie shook her head in amazement. This guy had nerve, moving her body about like a ragdoll just because he could, and talking to her like she was a naughty little girl. Unbelievable.

"I wonder how the owner of this ranch would feel if he knew how you're treating his new business partner," she said, barely able to contain her anger.

He slowed the horse to a halt. "What did you say?"

His voice was steely, even, and the hint of threat behind the words made Allie slink back—only to be reminded by the feel of his arm around her that she was quite literally not going anywhere.

"I didn't mean…" She swallowed hard, and forced herself to meet his hard gaze. "I have a meeting with Bill Edwards. I just was looking for him, that's all."

"*I* am Bill Edwards," he said. "And you can bet your bottom dollar I was not expectin' you."

Any dream she'd had of impressing her new business partner with her professionalism flew out the window. Her hopes of seeing Bill in person and instantly picking up where their emails had let off were dashed as well. She looked heavenward and sighed audibly.

"Can we start over?" she asked, still looking at the impossibly panoramic sky.

"Allie Crawford," he said, not answering her question. "Live and in the flesh."

Allie dropped her gaze and looked at him, trying to behave the same way she did with the stallion. *Don't show any sign of fear, and act in a non-threatening way.* Whatever she'd thought she knew about Bill Edwards had to go on the backburner now that she had the *real* Big Bad Bill in front of her. This cowboy was as wild as his horse—his reputation had preceded him, and she should've known it was him.

"I know what you're thinking," she said, her throat scratchy from when she'd screamed. "But it's still me. You…know me."

"I suppose the contract's already signed," he grumbled, "and I have to trust you with my uncle's diner. You better be as good as you say you are."

"I am." Allie lifted her chin, trying to look like she meant it.

It was hard to feel confident balancing so precariously on the saddle, with this man—this man she'd stupidly thought was her *friend*—who acted like he hated her at the same time as he held her tightly against him, whether she wanted him to, or not.

And she better be as good as she said she was…or what?

This was a mistake.

Bill jumped off the horse; his long, thick leg, clad in denim, swung around with surprising agility for a man his size. Without waiting for Allie to climb down, he reached up to take her around the waist and pulled her off the horse. She slid against his body for one terrifying second before her feet hit the ground.

"What day is it, anyway?" he growled.

"I know I'm early," she said. "But that's how it is. I need to stay in the apartment above the diner."

"No."

"It's mine," she said. "That's part of the *already-signed* contract."

The contract was exactly what she'd needed, broke as she was. She'd bought fifty percent ownership of the diner, and full ownership of the apartment above it, with the understanding that she would renovate, open and run the diner on her own, while Bill would put in one hundred percent of the money to get it open again. Then they would split the profits.

Seeing as how she'd drained her savings to buy half of the diner, she had nothing left to do any fixes or even to buy herself new clothes. The situation was really the only one she could've done. It was the only way to run her own diner, to have her own stake in it.

And now she'd just made her life-time, ongoing business partner hate her.

"Don't just stand there," he said roughly. "Let's go."

* * *

Allie closed the door of his farmhouse office behind her, and stood, waiting for an invitation to seat herself. It never came.

Bill leaned against the edge of his desk and looked down at her from his considerable height. His cool gray eyes studied her. Allie held her breath and stared back.

Oh my word, he's good-looking. And intimidating.

"You're really Allie, huh?" Bill said. "Thought you'd be…older."

"I thought the same of you," she said, and shrugged.

"How do ya like the middle of nowhere?"

It didn't matter whether she liked the location or not. It was the only diner she could afford—the only one with the unusual deal terms Bill offered—and the perfect excuse to get out of Miami. But she wasn't going to say that.

Allie put on a big smile. "This is the most beautiful place I've ever visited," she said. It was true, even if it wasn't her main reason for wanting the diner. "I'm very excited, and based on the pictures you sent of the diner—"

"—Zach Walker took those pictures," he interrupted. "Back when my uncle was still running the place."

Allie nodded. So the pictures were old. She kind of already knew that, or did she? Had she looked past that little tidbit when they were exchanging info online?

"Your assistant took great photos," she offered.

"Zach ain't my assistant," he said. "Those ranch hands pretty much run the place now."

"I'm sorry," she said. *Stop apologizing.* A man wouldn't apologize.

"It's better for me that way," he replied, mistaking her apology for calling Zach an 'assistant' as sympathy. "I don't have any time to do what I used to do 'round here on the ranch. May as well get this straight right now—all that emailin', I don't have time for that much involvement in real life. Runnin' that diner is all on you. "

If he didn't run the ranch, and he couldn't run the diner, what exactly did he *do* all day?

"Of course," she said, and smoothed her slacks, which had taken a beating from the stallion incident. "I understand completely. You don't want to be...involved."

Bill looked at her, concern showing in his eyes that hadn't been there before. "Did you hurt yourself when you fell?"

"I only hurt my pride," she admitted, "and my one chance at meeting you on a good note."

He shook his head. "You talk jus' like you write. It's strange hearin' the words come outta your mouth."

"Right?" Allie laughed. "Maybe it would be easier for us both if we just pulled out our phones and started emailing each other instead. Just pretend we never met and immediately started screaming at each other."

Bill smiled, finally, his first smile at her since she'd finally laid eyes on him. His whole face brightened, his straight white teeth contrasting handsomely with the dark scruff on his jaw.

Well, her phone was missing, but it was a good plan.

"I'd like to get started fixing up the diner right away," she added. "You don't have to do anything."

"Have at it," he said, and tossed a set of keys to her.

They dropped to the floor by her feet, since she wasn't expecting the cowboy to just randomly throw things at her.

"Oops…thank you," she muttered, and picked them up. "Do you have a checkbook you can throw at me too?" Allie jingled the keys to the diner as if it would distract him from the uncomfortable discussion of money. "Seriously though."

"You just got here," Bill said, "and you already want access to my checking account?" He glared at the keys as if he might rip them away from her, right out of her hand.

She gripped the keys in her sweaty palm, silencing them. The man crossed his arms in front of his muscular chest and raised an eyebrow.

"As per our arrangement," she reminded him through gritted teeth. "I need a checkbook or a debit card to an account that exists solely for business expenses, or whatever you think is best so I can get out of your hair. Either way, the sooner this diner opens, the sooner we can start sharing the profits, right?"

Fifty percent profits on his family diner was a lot more than zero, which he was currently earning from the property. And until his additional investment for renovations was paid back, he'd actually be making *sixty-five* percent. Way more than zero.

Bill grunted. "Fine." He paused, staring out the big window to the hay field. "Suppose it's 'bout time my uncle's diner was opened back up," he said. "Been meaning to do it for a while now, but…" His voice dropped off.

"I understand," Allie said. "It must've been hard to think about taking on such a huge project while you were still mourning your uncle… and… your wife."

Bill's eyes flashed as he swiveled his head to face her, his jaw hardening. "Whatever you think you know about Melody," he said. "You don't know. Don't talk about her."

Allie's cheeks burned. She'd screwed up royally for the second time in…oh, twenty minutes? They'd just met—had she thought they were going to become best friends in only a few moments, especially after he'd thrown her over his horse with every intention of kicking her off his ranch?

Yup, she'd thought exactly that.

"I didn't mean to offend you," she whispered. "Sometimes I talk too much and say the wrong thing. I apologize."

Bill didn't respond.

She pulled her shoulders back and shook her head to clear the tension inside her. If only she could clear the tension in the room.

"Do you have time now to take me to see the diner?" she asked. It would probably be best to get back to talking business before she stuck her foot in her mouth again. "I'd love to see it in real life."

Bill nodded mutely, his jaw clenching. He grabbed his black cowboy hat off the hook by the door, and set it on his head. He grabbed the keys to his truck.

"Let's go," he said. "I don't have all day."

Allie groaned inwardly and followed him.

"I have to grab my phone," she said.

He glared at her and she just shook her head. What else could she do?

This was not how she'd imagined her first meeting with Bill Edwards. She'd wanted to impress him, to show him that she was worthy of his investment in her, and worth his faith in her.

He had to have faith in her if he intended to pay for her to renovate and open the diner, right? After all, if he felt it needed to stay in the family, that had to mean that he considered her worthy of helping him do that. Right?

Meeting Allie today must have been a big disappointment for him.

Well, forget that—she'd prove him wrong, too. Bill Edwards may be an ornery guy, but she was going to run the most fun, family-friendly, profitable diner in the whole county—whether Bill thought she could do it or not.

He'd signed a contract with her. So it didn't matter how much she angered him—he'd better stand up to his end of the bargain.

She just wanted him to hand her a stupid checkbook and stay out of her way. It would be easy enough to forget she'd ever thought she knew him. That she ever liked him, when he was still only a ping in her inbox. Allie had a diner to open and a new life to begin—and no tall, handsome cowboy with too much money and a bad attitude was going to stop her.

Chapter Three

ALLIE FOLLOWED BEHIND Bill as he led the way to the gravel parking area outside the farmhouse office. His long strides were too fast for her to keep up, which meant her current view of him was of only his back, his shoulder muscles flexing through his shirt as his arms swung with determination. Her gaze dropped past the untucked shirt and his denim-clad legs to a pair of scuffed black cowboy boots.

"So," Allie said, rushing up until she stood by his side. He unlocked his truck with a click of a button on his keychain. "I appreciate that you're taking me to see the diner. I know you're a very... busy man."

Bill scowled at her from under his black hat, as if he couldn't tell if she were being facetious or not. She didn't know either. Maybe he *was* busy? Or maybe he was just busy being alone.

"But I need to get down to business for a sec," she continued. "I've given you a rather large sum of money, Bill. We signed a contract. I own half of the diner. And since I'm the one that's meant to get this diner open and running again, I just want to make sure we're starting on the right foot."

Bill leaned in toward her, until her back was a mere fraction of an inch from the shiny black pickup truck door. He moved slowly, as if—now, unlike moments earlier—he had all the time in the world.

His face was close to hers. Uncomfortably close? Allie opened her mouth to ask him to say something (anything!), but he stopped her by opening the door she was leaning against with his long arm.

"Ridin' in the truck works better when you actually get in the vehicle," Bill said. "Little trick I picked up."

Allie snorted, unable to suppress her amusement at his dry tone, even if he didn't deserve a reaction. "I'll remember that."

The truck was so tall she had to grab onto the handle in the doorway frame and pull herself up. She looked out to Bill, who was still holding the door open for her, waiting for her to get situated.

"All settled now? All right then." He slammed the door, with a loud noise that made her jump.

He strode around to the other side of the truck wordlessly and climbed in with much more ease than she had. She couldn't help but to look over at him, at the hard lines of his face, at the steel in his eyes as the engine revved.

They rode off the property, down the long driveway that connected to a dirt road. When they got out of the ranchland, the connecting road was barely wide enough to let two cars pass. Unlike in busy Miami, no painted lines marked the streets. The mountains rose up around her, covered in evergreen trees, and the fields below teemed with horses, sheep, and cattle. They passed children playing in their yards, riding old bicycles that had probably been hand-me-downs from a few generations past, by the looks of them.

Several properties had trailers on them, tiny mobile homes with cheery awnings outstretched before them, and dogs guarding chicken coops on the lawn. In Miami, it was rare for the people who lived in trailers to own their land, but these people apparently had lots of land. They put more money into the huge shops, barns, and livestock than they did to their own abodes.

"The diner's out a ways," Bill said.

"In town, right?"

She should have made the trip out to Idaho to see the property before purchasing it, for sure—but if she'd done that, she would have been several hundred dollars short of the purchase price. Every penny counted.

"Every word I said in our emails was the truth," Bill said, "if that's what you're worried about. It's on one of our busiest corners in town. That's not saying much," he admitted, "since our downtown is small even by small town standards. But when Uncle Freddy had the diner open, it was the most well-visited place other than church."

Allie laughed with nervous excitement, then closed her mouth when he didn't even smile. "Can you tell me what the diner was like, in your Uncle Fred…um, Freddy's… time?"

Bill shrugged, keeping his eyes on the road ahead.

Maybe she'd asked the wrong question. But she wasn't just making idle conversation—knowing what the people in town would expect, what they were used to, and what they'd like in the future was important to her. Could be important to the diner's success… to *her* success.

"He kept it low key," Bill finally said, his voice quiet. "In the winter, it was warm and clean, and in the summer it was cool and clean. You could come in, sit down, order a coffee and some pie, an' no one would bother you."

"That sounds…" *Dull.* But she couldn't say that. She tried again. "That sounds quiet."

He turned his head to look at her. "Some of us like quiet."

"Not me."

"I noticed," he grumbled.

They pulled up to a stoplight at the intersection of Main Street and Huckleberry Road, the so-called busiest intersection in "downtown" Bear Creek Saddle. There were about six cars that she could see, parked in front of places of business. They were the only vehicle actually driving on the road.

Not a good sign… This town was deader than she'd imagined. Looking through the window of a butcher shop, she could see a man unloading some large game to be butchered. Weren't people supposed to go to the butcher to *buy* meat, instead of hand it over? And who had a whole shop just for a butcher, anyway? That was usually relegated to the back of the grocery store.

"Is it always like this?" she asked.

"Don't worry… you'll get your customers." Bill looked over to her, and once again she was struck by how good-looking he was. "We ranchers like our pie."

"That's good!"

"There's pretty much nothing to do here," Bill added. "The diner always had kinda a…captive audience."

Allie smiled to cover up for the butterflies fluttering in her stomach. If Bill kept looking straight at her, she might have to close her eyes. It was that intense.

"What's your favorite kind of pie?" she asked. "Wait—don't tell me."

She had an uncanny knack for guessing what dishes people

might enjoy eating. It made her a good waitress, and hopefully it would be a silly icebreaker as a way to get to know the new townsfolk in her diner. Well… *their* diner.

"I'm guessing you're a pecan pie type of man," she said, with way too much confidence.

He started to look away, unimpressed, and she backpedaled.

"No, wait!" Goodness, she was rusty. She lowered her volume. "Forget pie—you like *eggs*. Three eggs over-easy and a side of toast, no butter."

Bill grunted and raised his eyebrows.

"Am I right…did I get it?"

He didn't reply as they pulled into the back parking lot—really just a square of asphalt tucked behind the diner, and came around to open her door for her.

"This is it," Bill said.

He extended his arm for her to grab hold of him, and she jumped out of the truck. His hand was surprisingly large, and warm. The calluses spoke of a lifetime of working on the ranch. But the pain in his eyes… he was broken.

Completely broken.

Allie looked at him and tried to smile. Her new diner was a small, one story building, made out of cement blocks that had been stucco'd over and whitewashed.

"Plenty of folks park here, an' enter through the back way there," Bill said, pointing to an old door with the paint peeling from it.

A chain, meant to keep the door locked, instead hung limp at the side of the doorframe.

"Oh no," she gasped. "Did someone break in?"

"Well," Bill said, "the usual. Happens when any building is abandoned. Kids think it's their new clubhouse. I did it back in my day too, so I can't blame 'em."

"A clubhouse," she repeated.

"Even the older guys, they sometimes go in to meet up since it's convenient."

Allie nodded, determined not to make it into a big deal. If even the owner of the diner didn't care that kids had probably vandalized the inside of his uncle's diner, then why should she? For goodness' sake, Bill probably joined those guys hanging out in his diner. A private party of sorts.

Everything had to be fixed up and painted anyway.

"Come on," Bill said.

He put his hand on the small of her back to lead her. The intimacy of the gesture took her by surprise—especially since back at his office, he seemed to be doing everything he could to avoid even looking at her.

His touch warmed her skin through her blouse. It was bold of him, but either Bill wasn't aware of that, or didn't care. He led Allie—his hand still on her—to the front entrance that came in off the sidewalk. Next-door to the diner was a bank. That was good, maybe folks would cash their paychecks and grab dinner out.

The front window had been boarded over.

"Is there glass behind that board?" she asked.

Bill cocked his head to the side. "Broken glass. They're all broken. The boards are what's new." He pointed to some charred wood piled up by the side of the building. "That's from a little fire that broke out inside last month. Not sure how that happened."

Allie turned to him in exasperation. "This was your Uncle

Freddy's diner. Don't you care? This was his livelihood and you haven't even *maintained* it."

Bill looked down at her from his height advantage, his steel gray eyes staring into hers with an intensity that burned her like fire.

He took his hand off of the small of her back, and she missed it immediately.

"I don't know how they work things in *Miami*," he said, saying the name of the city as if it were an insult, "but I don't know who on earth you think you're talkin' to. Don't you scold me like I'm some naughty kid you wanna put in time-out."

This was all wrong. It wasn't supposed to go like this. Her first day with her new business partner—how had she already messed up so royally?

She shouldn't say anything more. But as Bill had already witnessed, staying quiet had never been her strong suit. No reason to change now.

"You owned this diner long before I bought in," she said, anger creeping into her voice. "You had an obligation to take care of it. Even if you couldn't run the business, how hard is it to keep it locked up and safe?"

"I told you the place needed fixin' up. You're acting like I lied to get you to buy in." He took his cowboy hat off and ran his large hand through his black hair with frustration.

"Repairs are coming out of *your* wallet," she snapped. "You led me to think you'd closed up the diner right as your uncle left it, and waited till now to reopen, with my help."

"Yeah," he said. "That's what happened."

"I knew it needed fresh paint, new flooring maybe, cosmetic fixes. You didn't tell me you and your buddies were sneaking back in and treating it like a clubhouse. That kids were breaking windows for fun." As if of their own accord, her gestures got bigger, accusatory. "Or was that *you* breaking those windows?"

Bill grabbed her hand from out of his face, and held her wrist captive. "You're actin' like you're gonna poke my eyes out, and I can't have that."

No one had ever restrained her before, or stopped her from getting in their space. Not that she usually did that. This man, this rancher…he brought out the intensity in her. None of it made sense. In that moment, she didn't know if she hated him, or respected him for standing up against her outburst.

Allie instinctually knew that if she'd calm down, get out of his face and back off, he wouldn't still be holding her wrist. Instead, she clawed at his hand with her free one, until he took hold of her other wrist as well.

"Get off me!" she yelled. She looked around the empty street. Could people see? There was no one, just her and Bill Edwards.

"Stop actin' like you're ready to fight me," he said, stepping in close, his breath hot on her cheek. Her hands were trapped between his broad, muscular chest, and her own body. "Stop screaming at me." He looked her straight in the eyes. "You should be a redhead with all that fire in you. On the phone, in emails, you seemed calm, organized, like you had your act together."

"I do," she said. "You don't know me."

"I'm gettin' to."

Ugh. It was true. He was getting to know the part of her she'd hoped to keep hidden—the part that was scared to death about taking on a project this huge on her own. The part of her that worried she wasn't going to be able to move on and make a life for herself without her ex-husband.

"What are you gonna do now, Allie?" Bill slowly, carefully, relaxed his grip on her wrists. He slid his hands up to cradle her own. "You gonna back out now?"

Chapter Four

"NO," SHE WHISPERED. "I'm not going to back out. Running this diner is my future. This has to work."

"It will," he said. "What's done is done. Uncle Freddy was another father to me. Losin' him was—" Bill shook his head, as if to stop himself from saying too much. "I didn't think of it as ruining his livelihood. I just didn't stop folks who still wanted to use the place, 'cause we all missed it. We missed *him*."

His anger before, she knew, was a thin veneer over the pain he had felt when his uncle had passed. And the passing of his wife not too long before that...

"Let's go inside," she said.

"All right. But if you start scoldin' on me again we're gonna have a problem."

She shook her head, just enough to acknowledge him. Yes, he was acting like a jerk, but he'd been through a lot. And maybe, judging by the sorrow he exuded behind his don't-mess-with-me façade, he was still going through it.

"Go on in," he said. "Door's...unlocked."

She held up the key he had tossed at her back in his office. "Guess these were just ceremonial, then."

Bill shrugged. "You looked like the kinda girl who means to keep things locked up." He smiled—a glimpse of the man she knew from his emails.

"Okay then," she said simply. "Let's do this."

Please don't be a complete tear-down.

The door opened with a creak. *Fix noisy door*, she noted.

Inside the diner, white sheets covered chairs, which had been stacked up like small barricades around the room. Where had those chairs been situated? There were no *tables* that she could see.

The kitchen took up the back half of the diner. The counters were worn, and the cooktop too was covered in white sheets, to keep the thick layer of dust that had accumulated on the sheets off of the appliances.

Above, the shelves for the pots and pans held various random items instead: a rifle; a small pile of matchbooks; a football, worn with age.

"Where'd all the kitchen supplies go?" Allie asked. "I mean, when your uncle died, wasn't this place still running and stocked? Did someone steal everything?"

"No," Bill said. "Nothin' like that." He gave her a look from under his hat. "We didn't sneak in and borrow it, either."

She widened her eyes innocently, as if that wasn't exactly the thought that had gone through her mind.

"Uncle Freddy got sick about a year before he died," Bill explained. "The diner closed when he had to take an early retirement. He sold everythin' he could to pay for his medical expenses. That's why all the tables are missin', and half the chairs. There used to be booths, too. It used to be a good place to sit and eat."

"How come he didn't sell the diner himself?" she asked.

Bill looked at her like she was crazy. "This is the family diner. It belongs in the family. That's why he left it to me—he wanted me to take over right then an' there, but I couldn't. Not with me an' Melody having…problems. I was just trying to do right by my wife."

His face stilled, as if he had said too much.

"You probably have enough money to not need to take on a partner like me," Allie said, walking around the diner, studying every detail. "I imagine you could have taken your money and renovated it yourself, and hired a cook and waitress to manage it on your behalf—without giving up your full ownership." She nudged a chunk of plaster with her foot before looking at him. "Why take me on? Why give me half the diner?"

Bill shrugged. "I'm busy," he said again. "I have no interest in running the diner. The only interest is in keepin' the diner going, with me as one of the owners so that it remains in the family. Someone like you—someone who is excited and willin' to work to make this happen—that's what the diner needed more than anything."

His unexpected appraisal filled her with courage. Bill knew that this diner, this business, meant everything to her. That failure was simply not an option.

He needed her motivation as much as she needed his money to make it happen. Was it a fair trade? Only time would tell.

"Hey," he said brusquely. "I'll get ya the checkbook tomorrow. You can use it to get what you need. But if you're gonna spend a big amount, run it by me first."

"What's a big amount?" she countered.

"Somethin' with more than a couple zeros," he said, as if he didn't care that much after all. "I don't know, get off my tail."

That man was hardly a charmer. It took considerable effort to not roll her eyes like a teenager. Speaking of…

Allie looked at the floor in the corner of the diner, where kids had stamped out cigarettes on the cement beneath the peeling linoleum. Someone had written on the wall with a black Sharpie: *RIP FRED, in HEAVEN!!!!!*

"So is this diner still being used as a 'clubhouse?'" she asked, staring at the graffiti.

"Prob'ly." He shrugged, like it didn't matter. "Ain't no diner in town to meet at."

Bill pulled the corner of the dusty white sheet off the edge of the main counter top by where the check register should've been. The wood was dull after a year of neglect. Allie wanted to rush right toward it to polish it and make it shine.

It would be awesome if she could wave a magic wand and make the entire diner just *poof!* transform into the one in her vision— bright and shiny and clean. But that transformation wasn't going to happen immediately, no matter how hard she wished. It would take time and effort. That's why she was there, anyway. It made *her* worth the investment Bill was making in the business.

Bill hopped up on to the counter with the ease of man accustomed to mounting horses, and sat, kicking his legs out in front of him, and let his boots thud against the side of the wall when they dropped.

"Have a seat, Allie," he said, patting the space next to him

She eyed him warily. "Why are you being nice to me, all of a sudden?"

They'd need to purchase some bar stools to put next to the counter, where people could order a soda and wait to be seated on busy nights. She left the graffiti behind and hopped up on to the counter next to Bill.

"Nice jump, there." The corner of his lips turned up in an almost-smile.

"Who are you, and where did that surly man go who was harassing me two minutes ago?"

He touched his cowboy hat, pulling the black rim down over his forehead just a bit more. "I don't feel like being 'surly' at the moment."

"Okay…" Allie raised her eyebrows. Guess she should just enjoy it while it lasted.

"I haven't been in here since Uncle Freddy retired," Bill said. "I didn't go look at it after he died either. Too many memories."

"What's it like being here now?" Allie asked.

"Nothin' like I remember it." He turned to her, his fingertips touching hers, splayed on the counter. "You gotta get everything back the way it was, Allie. Man, if I could go back two years…" A cloud came over his face.

The muscles in his thigh hardened against her own thigh, tensing. She was sitting too close; how did that happen? He was like a magnet, drawing her toward him.

"What would you do," she asked, urging him to finish his thought, "if you could go back in time?"

"Ne'er mind that," Bill said abruptly, as if he hadn't brought it up himself. "You can't go back in time. You can only move forward."

As if sensing that the conversation had turned too deep, too fast, Bill leapt from the countertop, his black boots hitting the cement floor. Allie froze, perched on the top of the counter.

Bill moved toward her and put his hands on her waist possessively, as if he thought that was appropriate.

"Bill," she whispered, the word barely coming out.

"I'm helpin' you down," he said quietly. "I didn't mean to scare ya."

"You don't scare me," she said, almost as if she meant it. "And I don't need help."

Getting up onto the counter had been easier than getting down would be, though. Why not accept a helping hand, especially when the helping hand was attached to Bill?

"Well, as my partner in this business venture," Bill said, "you won't be much use to me if you break an ankle your first day on the job."

Carefully, as if to avoid manhandling her the way he had on the horse, he lifted her from her waist like she weighed nothing, and set her feet lightly on the floor. He had touched her as if she were a breakable doll, instead of a sack of potatoes the way he'd done when his stallion was about to trample her. Who knew those big hands of his could be so gentle?

Whoa.

"Thank you," she said. Maybe he wouldn't notice her flushed cheeks.

The testosterone came off him in waves, intoxicating her. He cocked his head, his black hat shading his gray eyes as he stared into hers.

The air was thick with sudden tension.

"Come on," he said, his voice low. He put his large, warm hand on her lower back, guiding her back toward him with gentle but firm pressure. "I haven't even shown you your apartment."

For a moment, she faltered. Allie felt an internal pull toward this cowboy—not even necessarily the Bill she'd gotten to know from his emails, but also *this* Bill…one moment cold, the next hot, broken and vulnerable… this man whose very touch made her tremble. *Wait—no.*

They shouldn't even be in the same room as each other right now, much less in her new living quarters.

"We've just…" Allie breathed, gathering her thoughts from wherever her hormones had discarded them. "I know it feels like we know each other, but really we've only just met."

No matter how attractive he is. Besides, he was Big Bad Bill. The last thing she needed was for a man to swoop into her life and spin everything upside-down again.

A look of confusion crossed his face for a split-second, and then he smirked. "Maybe it's 'cause it only 'feels like we know each other'," he said, "but I got a pretty good idea of what you thought I was suggestin'."

"But you weren't," she guessed.

He grinned. "I'll stay down here, then, while you go check out your new apartment upstairs on your own."

Oh. Right.

"Yes," she said, "that's for the best."

She sighed. He must think she was a fawning school girl. Obviously he'd only intended to show her around upstairs. Any romantic tension in the air had dissipated. Maybe it had never been there in the first place.

"I suppose you could…wait at the bottom of the stairs for me," she said. "In case I have any questions, I mean."

"Of course." He touched his hat, but in a way that seemed like he was appeasing her social awkwardness, like a mockery of chivalry.

Seemed he felt like being mean again. Their period of détente hadn't lasted long.

Allie walked over to the door in the back of the diner and opened it. A long skinny staircase went up into the darkness.

"So this leads to the apartment above the diner?" she asked.

Bill nodded. "It's all yours. I haven't been up there since I had to gather my uncle's things and move 'em out."

She reached her hand into the darkness, her fingers brushing blindly against the wall until the hard plastic of the light switch nudged her hand.

She turned around and looked at Bill. "Can't you turn on the power or something?"

"Don't look at me like that," he said, raising one thick eyebrow. "You're the one who showed up two weeks early."

Right.

"Is that a no?" Allie crossed her arms in front of her chest. Going up into that dark apartment with no lights was…scary.

"It's a 'gimme some time and I'll have it sorted,'" he shot back without missing a beat. "But you'll be fine goin' up there on your own, you said so yourself." He chuckled to himself. "Go on, now."

Allie growled under her breath, and opened the flashlight app on her phone. It was horrible for her battery, but it worked like a charm. The stairs creaked as she climbed them, putting each foot lightly on the wood before letting her full weight rest, in case the stairs broke.

They shouldn't break, of course. Why would they? But the building had such a rundown feel, stepping lightly seemed like a valid choice.

Bill wasn't following her. She almost wished he would, after all. As large and growly as he was, the shadows here made the hair on the back of her neck stand up.

Stop that.

"Yea though I walk through the valley of the shadow of death, I shall fear no evil," she whispered under her breath. The familiar cadence of the biblical verse took her calmly up the rest of the creaking steps.

She shined her flashlight-app around, and the sound of tiny claws on linoleum scattered. Something scurried away along the wall. She covered her mouth, muffling the unexpected squeal of disgust.

Mice. Or rats! (*No, no, imagine it's just a cute little mouse from a kid's animated movie*). But imagining those mice (*rats?*) singing and dancing on their hind legs didn't work, or make her feel any less creeped-out.

The stairs opened up to a small main room with a couch. Cotton stuffing from the couch littered the carpet, and the middle cushion had a spring sticking out, glinting off the light from her cell phone. Somewhere underneath the beer cans, cigarette butts, and old newspapers, was a coffee table… at least she assumed there was a coffee table. Surely it wasn't just a pile of junk?

While the couch faced the wall, as if there would have been a TV there…there was no TV. Someone must've taken it. Someone from town?

Nah—in a town this small, it wouldn't make sense for a local to steal from another local. The chance of getting caught was way too high. Maybe it was an outsider, an out-of-towner.

Not an out-of-towner like herself, of course. Allie would be different. She hadn't come all the way to Bear Creek Saddle to cause trouble, or even to change the way folks did things.

(*Except for their*—our—*local diner*). Change was coming for that, for sure.

Something scratched in the walls and she shuddered. Unbelievable of that man, allowing his own building to go to the dumps like this.

The one bedroom consisted of a mattress on the floor, and nothing else. Where had all the furniture gone? It appeared people had just taken things out of the apartment—*her* apartment! —as they saw fit.

"Not cool," she muttered.

Bill had promised it would be furnished—and considering she couldn't exactly go purchase a whole bunch of furniture (or even a microwave), she'd been pretty much counting on that.

Had homeless people been squatting here, or maybe transients traveling through, on their way to Canada, maybe? Was it just the good old boys in town, commandeering the place as their own? Perhaps the teenagers gathered here to have some privacy from their folks. Surely Uncle Freddy wouldn't have sold the furniture out from under himself while he was still alive.

Light from a window in the bathroom gave her a good look at the yellowing tile, the dirty tub and everything else. That wasn't a surprise since the water had been shut off to the building. She pulled her shirt up to cover her nose and mouth.

Note to self: buy latex gloves, and bleach. And a Hazmat suit.

The emerald-green blouse she'd worn to impress stuck to her sweaty skin. Heels had been a bad choice to wear, especially when her "business meeting" took place bottom-up over a horse.

Had she really thought she could change her stripes so fast? As much as she'd dreamed about owning her own diner, her own place, and running a business…it meant nothing when faced with cold, hard reality. And reality was getting harsher by the millisecond.

Allie had no idea what she was doing, and it wouldn't be long before everyone else knew it too. She'd given up her old life in Miami, driven across the country, and drained her savings… for *this*.

"I'm toast."

Lord, help me turn this around.

Chapter Five

ALLIE SWALLOWED HARD, a trick she'd learned to keep from letting how upset she was show on her face. It didn't always work. At least Bill wasn't there to witness how freaked out she was by the apartment she now owned.

"'Good condition, needs TLC,' yeah right," she muttered.

She'd been counting on the apartment to be in at least livable condition. She didn't need anything fancy. In fact, when Bill had told her that she could stay in the apartment above the diner once she fixed it up, she'd been under the impression that if she were willing to live in a less-than-ideal place, that she'd be fine to stay there.

You know, *now.*

Ugh. He'd even told her she'd probably want to find someplace better to stay for the first couple of weeks, until she'd made her apartment suited to her liking.

How could she not have listened to him, or at least not been so fixated that she couldn't hear what he meant?

"I have nowhere to sleep tonight," she whispered, her voice bringing some normalcy to the eerie silence in the room.

Allie traced her steps back out of the bathroom, through the living room and took a quick look into the kitchen: a refrigerator, a tiny stove, and an empty spot where a microwave had once been. She didn't dare open the refrigerator—there was no telling what she'd find (or smell).

Hey, at least there's still a fridge. Small blessings, right?

Behind her, the floor creaked…a painful sound, as if old bones grinded against each other.

Allie froze, all her senses on high alert.

There was something in the room… a presence. The hairs on the back of her neck stood on end. A chill ran down her spine.

"…Uncle Freddy?" she whispered.

"It's me," Bill's low voice said from behind her.

She whirled around, staring at his silhouette in the living room. "I didn't really think you were your uncle," Allie said quickly, embarrassed. "I just got confused in the dark."

Confused enough to momentarily believe in ghosts, apparently.

Bill shrugged. "You've been up here for a while."

Allie looked around the place in desperation. Tears filled her eyes, and she tilted her head back so they wouldn't fall down her cheeks. Not in front of Bill—it was too unprofessional to let herself be so vulnerable in front of him.

Her whole day with Bill she'd been the epitome of unprofessional.

But she couldn't stay here. Even with electricity and water turned on she wouldn't be able to stay at her apartment until it was at least up to code—she could tell even with her untrained eye that it was uninhabitable.

"There's quite a bit of work to do up here," she said. *Understatement of the year.*

Thank goodness it was dark…hopefully he wouldn't see the tear that rolled down her cheek—the one that got away from her. She felt helpless and stupid enough as it was.

The flashlight app on her cell phone crashed, and the phone went dark.

She groaned under her breath. The battery had died. Without any light, and the main window boarded over, the room was thrown into pitch black.

"I want to go back downstairs," she said. Something scurried past her. "I want to go downstairs *now*."

"All right," Bill said softly. It was the most gentle thing he'd said yet, the tone of it.

Bill reached out for her in the darkness and took her hand in his. The unexpected contact made her breath catch. His hand was large, his fingers warm.

"I'm right here," Bill said.

His hand on hers was a welcome anchor in the sea of darkness. The stairs, she knew, were only a few feet in front of her, and went down quite steeply. Would she fall?

Bill gave her hand a slight tug. "Come on," he said. "I've got you."

Allie stumbled forward, right against Bill's broad, muscular chest.

"I'm sorry!" she gasped. "I'm all over the place today."

"Follow right behind me," Bill said. "If you fall, you'll fall on me."

He almost made it sound like a good thing.

She shuffled closely behind him, her hand gripping his.

"First step," Bill warned.

They went down the stairs at a snail's pace. At the end at the landing, Bill pushed open the door into the diner.

Allie was so grateful to be out of that apartment, she could've kissed the dirty cement floor at her feet. Instead, she turned around and looked at him, unable to hide her anger.

"Y-you've *misled* me," she said, her voice shaking. "I can't believe I actually paid money for this dump. A lot of money. *All* my money."

The long hours in the car, the humiliation of falling over her own feet and having Bill toss her over his saddle—combined with sheer disillusionment—came to a head. Tears that had been building up in her all day finally fell, and she leaned up against the dusty wooden counter in exhaustion.

"Whoa, there." Bill took a step back, crossing his arms as if to barricade himself from her. "I didn't 'mislead' anyone," he said firmly. "I sent you pictures of everythin' in detail. Complete descriptions. You signed a contract that said AS-IS."

"I never saw pictures of *that!* It looks like it was taken over by a group of hobos or something!" she said, her voice rising. "I thought I could stay here while I was fixing everything up. Clearly that is not the case."

The muscle in his jaw hardened.

"You should have warned me," she added.

Each verbal jab at Bill made his jaw clench even tighter. Well, he could just be as angry at her as he wanted to be. It was a free country. But he'd better not dish out more than he could take, because right now, Allie was about two steps away from saying forget it—forget the whole thing.

"I can get the water and electricity back on," Bill said. "I can have the guys come in and take out the furniture that's no good. We'll call the plumber if we need to. It won't be pretty, but you could live here if you want to."

"Are you kidding me?" This time she didn't bother to moderate her volume. "I can't live here. And don't look at me like that—"

"—like what?"

"Like I'm some prissy city-girl," she said.

Bill raised his eyebrows and shrugged his shoulders. "You said it, not me."

"You can't be serious," she fumed. "If I went to sleep in that apartment, the mice would probably eat my face off. That is, if whatever plague is growing in that bathroom didn't get me first."

Bill didn't reply.

Ah. So now he was playing the cowboy-of-few-words. Seriously, that trait was annoying when she had to deal with it in person—even if it was attractive in a western movie. And she knew him better than that. He couldn't be as nonchalant about this as he pretended to be—so unruffled by her display.

"Anythin' else?" he finally asked.

Allie exhaled heavily and shook her head. But she couldn't leave it like this between them. He didn't act like he understood what she was feeling. Maybe he didn't even care.

No wonder they called him Big Bad Bill. Their first day together and he'd already reduced her to tears.

"I feel like I was duped," she said, looking directly in his eyes— making him *see* her. "I spent all of my money to do this. The only way that I could do this is because you are paying for the renovation. I've never even renovated anything before!"

The look on his face gave her pause. She'd told him that before, right?

At some point, she'd had to have come clean and mentioned that while she knew her way around a diner, she had zero experience with renovations. Or maybe not.

Well.

Secret's out.

Bill didn't look happy with her now, either. "You'd told me in an email that you've helped renovate your sister's house."

"I helped paint the walls, and I put up the curtains, all right? And before you ask, no, I didn't use the drill and attach the curtain rods. I literally just put the curtains on the rods." She smiled ruefully. "Are you happy?"

"No."

"I don't know how long it will take to renovate an entire apartment and diner," she admitted. "I wanted to renovate the diner first, so we could get it open and start making some money. I have no money anymore, nothing coming in. If I have to spend time renovating the apartment first, so I'll have somewhere to live, we're going to lose *weeks*." She sank to the floor of the diner, ignoring the gravel and chunks of plaster strewn about.

"Weeks, huh?" Bill said. "You'd have a point, if you actually knew what on earth you were doing."

"Which I don't."

"Nope." He stood above her, looking down at her from his immense height, and rubbed the stubble on his chin. "I bet we can get the apartment in shape sooner than you think," Bill said. "It'll get done. But you were right— the diner needs to be top priority so we can open."

"I needed to stay in the apartment here," she muttered. "None of my planning works if I don't have a free place to stay until this diner opens."

He shook his head. "It's your own fault—spendin' every last dollar on this venture. What were you gonna do for income till the diner was ready to go? Can't buy food an' gasoline with just a pretty face."

Perhaps he'd hoped to soften his words with his backhanded compliment. If so, it didn't work.

"I've brought lots of food with me," she said, her defenses rising. "Cans and cereal and stuff. I'll be fine for a little while at least."

"Right." He grunted in a way that Allie translated as "good luck with that."

Great.

"You could stay in the motel outside of town," Bill said. "Wasn't part of our deal, but I'd be willing to foot the bill for a short while so you can have a comfortable place to sleep until your apartment is…up to your standards."

She eyed him warily. Was he making fun of her about her "standards"? Seriously, "livable" was not a particularly high standard as far as she was concerned.

"I appreciate the offer," she said, "but no way. I mean—no thank you."

Bill frowned. "And here I stand, thinkin' that was a mighty fine offer."

"Even if you paid for it," she said, "it's a two-hour round-trip drive to and from the nearest motel. I don't even think I have enough gas to get out of Melody Ranch at this point. And I'm not wasting two hours driving every day, fourteen hours a week, when

I should be on site, working to make this happen!"

"Hey," he said, his voice firm.

Allie wanted to kick something in frustration. "No income until it does, remember?"

"Don't be raising your voice at me." He pushed his cowboy hat back and rubbed his forehead. "You've got no one to blame but yourself."

"The bottom line is, I need a place to stay that doesn't cost any money, and that isn't detrimental to my health and safety."

Bill cocked his head, as if waiting patiently for her to figure out a solution all by herself. It wasn't right, she was new in town. He owed it to her to set this right, for goodness' sake. Why couldn't he see that?

If she could email him and ask him for a place to stay, Allie would bet he'd jump on it. But here, outside the realm of the internet, real life got in the way. It made him different.

Or did it?

"You have that farmhouse," she suggested. "Maybe I could set up in there. Surely it has a bathroom if it used to be a proper house, right?"

"No way," Bill said sharply. "That's the main office for Melody Ranch. You can't stay there—it ain't some sort of guest house."

"Well, since you're such a 'big, bad' cowboy, a few mice and a mattress on the floor shouldn't scare you," Allie said. "You can stay in the apartment above the diner, and I'll trade you for your house." Sarcasm dripped from every word.

It didn't matter if he hadn't actually ripped her off. She *felt* ripped off, and she felt broke and stupid for giving up everything for a dream. How fitting that this would be what her dream looked like in reality. Broken glass and cigarette butts.

"All right." His face didn't betray any emotion.

"Bill…" She sighed. "Why won't you just invite me to crash on the couch at your house for a few days? We're not strangers, not really. Maybe it's me who's acting dumb—to think that after three months of emailing back-and-forth that we might actually… like each other." The last few words came out mumbled, quiet.

"You're not dumb," Bill said.

"I guess I really am a big disappointment to you," she said. "Maybe I'm not as great in person as I am in an email."

"No," Bill said. "I wasn't lookin' at you then…couldn't see your face. Couldn't see the emotion behind your words. Now I can."

Allie listened, needing to hear this. To know why she didn't have that immediate connection with Bill she'd expected, the kind of partnership where she'd drive up and he'd give her a hug, and they'd start up right where they'd left off. Instead, it was like they had to start from the beginning… despite knowing more about each other than a stranger should.

"I'm—I think you are a…an attractive woman," he said. "All right? You happy now?"

Allied considered. "I'm not sad."

Bill's mouth opened, as if he had to say something, but didn't know what.

"Maybe letting me stay at your house," she continued, "instead of making me stay in this disgusting apartment you've sold me, will go a long way toward renewing my faith and goodwill in you."

Now it was Allie who crossed her arms and waited.

"You wanna stay at my house, after I told you I'm attracted to you?" he asked in apparent surprise. "That doesn't worry you?"

"You're a grown man who is in full control of his own actions. I don't think you're going to hurt me."

He swallowed, his handsome face so vulnerable, yet so strong. "I would never hurt you," he said. "But I can't risk havin' my—" Bill stopped speaking abruptly.

"What can't you risk?" she whispered.

"Forget it," Bill said, his words barely audible, his lips barely moving. "You can stay at my house. But I need my space, and it's a small place. If you see me, leave me be."

Allie didn't know whether to laugh or cry. "Let me get this straight. I can stay in your house, but if I come out to make some coffee, and you're already in the kitchen, I have to turn around and go back to my room? Because…you need your space?"

(Or because he's attracted to me?)

It wasn't like she could afford to be choosey. It was either deal with a prickly man or sleep in her car—again. No thanks.

Bill took a step toward her, and stared down at her from where she sat on the ground. "That's right."

"Or maybe we could act like normal people, and sometimes be in the same room," she suggested. "Once in a while. Especially if I'm taking over your couch."

"I've got a spare room, and you'll have the whole place to yourself at night. Like you said, a few mice and a mattress on the floor don't scare me."

"Wait. What?"

"I won't be tradin' you my house, Allie. But I'll sleep here at the apartment until you're ready to move into it."

"I was just joking before, Bill—you can't sleep in this dump."

"This *dump* holds some good memories for me, at least."

Oh. She'd nearly forgotten it was his late uncle's former home. "I'm sorry, didn't mean it that way," she backtracked. "But the…the plumbing doesn't even work."

"No need for you to fuss. I just need to sleep here, that's all, an' I'll shower and eat at my home per the usual."

"Well…I mean…okay. Thank you," she said. Allie really hadn't been expecting him to take her up on her offer of trading sleeping locations. "I know it's your house. I won't mess anything up."

"I know," he said. "'Cause I'm gonna be there with you, every minute, 'cept for my 7 hours of shut-eye. I'll leave you be at 11pm and return at 6am, bright an' early."

"All this, just so your truck and my car won't be seen in the same driveway overnight together?" While she appreciated the sentiment greatly, it almost didn't seem fair to Bill at this point. "You'll still basically be having me as a house guest."

"You may not realize this, Miz Miami, but up here in Bear Creek Saddle, neighbors take note when a man's truck is parked next to a woman's vehicle overnight. Whether or not we're doing anythin' improper don't matter."

He was right. She'd gotten so accustomed to the liberal worldview everyone seemed to have in Miami, that she hadn't even thought about how her staying over at Bill's house could be perceived by others in a small, God-fearing town. Even though she knew for a fact she wasn't ready for anything more than a platonic friendship, they didn't know that.

"I'm trying to be a gentleman about this," he said, "so just let me."

Heat flushed her cheeks. Why was she fighting him on this? He was right, he'd be fine sleeping at the apartment for a while until things got fixed. Couldn't be worse than camping, right? And it was a visible way to let nosy townsfolk know they weren't having an inappropriate relationship.

That sort of thing hadn't mattered so much to her before, in Miami—she'd always figured as long as God knew what was going on, she'd be fine no matter what others believed. But Bill was right on this one. The perception of behavior as well as the actual behavior mattered.

"Okay," she said finally. "Thank you, Bill. I...really appreciate it. And I'll do what I can tonight to make the apartment more...um, less of a..."

"Right." Bill offered her his hand. She took it, his biceps flexing as he pulled her to standing. "We can get started right away."

"*We?*" Allie raised an eyebrow.

"Zach Walker's got the ranch covered tonight," he said, clearly misunderstanding the reason she was surprised he offered his help. "I'm not worried with him and the guys around."

"You're already doing more than you bargained for," she reminded him. "I don't need any help."

"So I'll just leave you here, then," he said.

It took her a moment to realize he was being sarcastic. He really didn't think she could handle it! Maybe he was right. But that didn't change the fact that she wanted to be in charge of the renovations. It was going to be *her* apartment, after all. And half of her diner.

"Let's not forget," she said, putting as much calm professionalism into her voice as possible "our contract states you pay for 100% of the renovations, but *I* am 100% responsible for making them happen. So. Maybe you could just...get out of my way, and I will get to work, by myself." She paused. "Your checkbook is your contribution, remember."

"Right," he said, a little smirk on his face. "You don't need me one bit, not with all your experience renovating places. I'll give you the number to get electricity and water turned back on."

As he rattled off the phone numbers, Allie grabbed at her phone to punch them in. "Hold up…goodness."

Right. Her completely dead phone.

"I need to go charge this," she sighed. "And then I can call."

"Come on," he said. "Let's go back to the ranch."

His hand on her back again—as if to guide her—was so intimate. Allie wasn't accustomed to having a man touch her so much, as if he couldn't help but to be physically drawn to her. Was it because their months of interaction meant they were already…close enough?

The energy he imparted made her shiver, tremble. If he noticed, surely he'd know how much he was affecting her.

Bill gave her a slow grin. "I was just messin' with you before—if you call those numbers, you'll get my phone. I'm who to call for electric an' water."

Allie laughed. "Aww, I ruined your prank. I bet you were looking forward to answering both phone calls from me, huh."

"I was," he laughed. "But I'll make sure everything is ready for tomorrow. I don't need power or water for tonight."

"Do I still have to call? Or does this count?"

"This counts." Bill brushed his hand over her hair.

"Hey," she whispered. What was that?

"Dust," he said. "I got it."

Allie swiped the plaster and dust from her clothing, pulled her shoulders back and nodded, not even mad he'd been playing games with her about the utilities. "Fine."

She was in way over her head. Now she had to coexist with Big Bad Bill for whatever twenty-four hours minus seven hours of sleep was. And he seemed to want nothing to do with her, except for when he did an about-face and *did* want her. Well, he'd just have to live with it. If he'd bothered to make sure the apartment he'd sold her was up to code, he wouldn't be having an unexpected houseguest inviting herself over.

Unless he'd planned it that way, so they'd spend more time together?

No. He couldn't have known she'd be showing up two weeks ahead of schedule.

Outside, Bill closed the chain on the door, and locked it. "We need to get somethin' straight."

Allie's stomach flipped, as if she'd gotten in trouble in school and had been sent to the principal's office. "Okay."

"You implied—whether you meant to or not—that you had experience renovatin'," he said. "You don't." He didn't sound as angry about it as she would have imagined he would be. "That part of the contract that says I'll stay out of your way...it's null and void now."

"What?" she asked. "No. That's not fair."

"I don't care if you think it's fair. I'm investin' a lot of money into this—into you. I'm gonna be here with you, every step of the way."

"Aren't you too busy with the ranch, anyway?" Allie asked, changing her tactic.

"My guys haven't needed me at the ranch for a while now. I can take a couple weeks off. But that ain't your concern. From now on, you're gonna live and breathe and dream about this diner. Got it?"

"You're a jerk," she muttered under her breath. Taking over, acting like he owned her.

He leaned down until his face was close to hers, as if to hear her better. "Go on."

"The pictures you emailed to me did *not* show this level of... neglect."

"The pictures are from when my uncle was still alive, all right? But you showed up two weeks early," Bill said. "I could've gotten the place cleaned up, at least, before you were supposed to be here. That's on you."

"It's all my fault, huh?" She rolled her eyes. "Why didn't you at least keep this place locked up? It was your responsibility! The whole time we were emailing, talking about the diner, about our future together as partners—the very future of your Uncle Freddy's diner—you couldn't bring yourself to mention even *once* that you'd let it all go to the dogs?"

Bill shook his head, and turned his back on her, walking right toward the door.

What on earth?! He couldn't just leave. Not when she had a bone to pick with him, a serious bone.

She ran to the door, crossing in front of him, and pressed her back against it, her arms splayed to keep him from leaving.

He stopped directly in front of her and crossed his arms, looking merely annoyed by her antics.

"Are you kidnapping me?" he asked. "Holdin' me hostage?"

"I think I have a few more hours before this could count as a kidnapping," she said. "But I'm willing to risk it. We can call the Sheriff and ask him later, after we figure out what we're going to do about this."

Bill sighed. "Have ya ever pretended something doesn't exist, 'cause maybe then it'll go away?"

"I'm not going away, Bill Edwards."

At that, he shook his head. "I couldn't pretend you didn't exist if I tried. But I did ignore my responsibility. I sold you the job of takin' care of renovations and day-to-day operations. It was the best I could do."

She paused, thinking of the disgusting bathroom upstairs, and the mice. "We need a plumber, and an exterminator. And you need to figure out what was stolen or damaged, write it down, and give me back my share of whatever it was. Cash."

"All right," he said slowly. "That's fair."

The expression on his face had gone from annoyed to... respectful? Did he respect her for sticking up for herself?

Well, good. It was something she'd have to do more of. Just like Ginger had said, she had to keep her chin up and not be scared of Big Bad Bill.

"Just so ya know," he added, "any damage or theft—that was done by people I don't know. Guys outside of town. The folks in Bear Creek Saddle would never disrespect Fred like that."

Allie pointed to the graffiti that said *RIP Fred In Heaven!!!* and raised her eyebrow.

Bill nodded. "That's not really vandalism... more of a... you know what I mean."

Let him think what he wanted about how the diner got to the state it was in. That didn't matter as much as the fact that she'd spent her life savings on a building she couldn't live in, and needed far more work to renovate than he'd represented to her.

At least she'd get some cash back because of this, something she needed even more than she'd realized she would.

Allie shook her head. "And just so *you* know, I already do live, breathe and dream about this diner. I have ever since I contacted you on Craigslist."

Her words must have softened him. He fingered the chain on the door, touching the cold metal with two long, calloused fingers.

"I should've taken better care of this place," he admitted, his voice low. "But we're gonna get everythin' back to the way it was. It's what we gotta do. What the town needs."

If their previous emails meant anything, then getting the diner back to the way it was sounded like something that *Bill* needed, whether the town needed it too, or not.

Allie didn't want everything to go back the way it was... She wanted her own vision, her own dream. Could they make it happen without killing each other first?

Bill Edwards, in person, bore little resemblance to the person he'd been online. In their emails, he'd been nice. Funny, even. He spoke well—or rather, *wrote* well —putting his thoughts out clearly to her. But in person, it was like he was being mean for no reason, as if out of habit.

Didn't he remember? They were already... friends. Weren't they?

Chapter Six

ALLIE FOLLOWED BILL down the gravel walkway that led up to his home. More like a log cabin, really. It was small, with beautiful hand-hewn logs and a wraparound deck. In the area he had appropriated as his backyard, a vegetable garden and chicken coop took up most of the space. Tall wire fences surrounded both.

"Hey, did your tomatoes ever grow back after the moose incident?" Allie asked, referring to one of his old emails.

"Yup," he said. "You shoulda seen that moose. She was so tall, she just bent her big head over the top of the wire there."

"Did you stop her?"

Bill laughed. "Moose aren't all that afraid of men. They know they're bigger; they'll just trample you if they want." He raised his arms high above his head, demonstrating just how huge moose were.

"Whoa," she said. "You're gargantuan yourself, Big Bad Bill, so if the moose was even bigger, that's scary."

He put his arm around her shoulders in an unexpected display of affection. "See, I like how it sounds when *you* say it."

She smiled up at him, not wanting him to move his arm away. If felt too good to be close to him. "Big, Bad, Bill…" she whispered, teasing.

"Little, Good, Allie," he replied with a wink.

This was what she liked, just talking with him, back and forth, no fighting, no agenda. When he wasn't actively trying to be mean to keep his distance, he was a really great guy.

The beautiful landscape around them, the mountains, the evergreens, the cabin and the chickens—it all disappeared. The only thing she could see was him, his handsome face as he looked down into her own.

It would be so counterproductive to her ambitions if she rushed their friendship into some sort of relationship. There was no way she'd be able to separate her feelings for him from the diner, and considering he was her partner in the diner, getting her heart broken again only a year after her husband left her—she couldn't let that happen. Any relationship trouble they'd experience if they became a couple could adversely affect their business.

And that diner—it was her chance.

"We have to be careful," she said. Gently, she put her hand on his chest and pressed.

If he hadn't agreed to move away, he wouldn't have budged. Pushing against him was like trying to move a mountain. But Bill was a gentleman, and dropped his arm from her shoulders immediately.

"I'm sorry, Allie," he said, concern flitting through his gray eyes. "Wasn't thinkin'."

She smiled and shook her head. "It's no big deal. We just have to put the business first."

"Right," he said. He stepped back, and gestured toward the house. "The diner comes first."

He led the way up to his front door, and glanced back at his vegetable garden. "I had to stand there like a fool waiting for that moose to finish up eatin' my tomatoes." He laughed.

"Tallest plant, easy pickin's," Allie said, mimicking some of his accent with a smile.

She shook her hands as if to dispel the romantic tension they'd built between them. *Don't think about gazing into his face like that again.*

For all she knew, he was just trying to distract her from the fact that he'd let her apartment and diner go downhill. That she was only there at his house in the first place, because he had royally misled her—even if it hadn't been on purpose.

Or maybe she had only heard what she wanted to hear—that she could live in the apartment right away.

Bill pushed open his unlocked front door—apparently locking up after himself was a foreign concept in general—and gestured her inside.

The interior of the cabin was warm and homey. From the entranceway, she could see the entire house, even the little kitchen off to the right. It was so small she couldn't imagine more than one person cooking in it at any time. An open area consisted of the living room and dining area, and what appeared to be bedrooms down a little hall.

"Nice place," she said.

"Built it with my own hands," he said, and smiled. Then, "Well, the guys helped quite a bit, too."

His teeth were white and straight, and his whole face brightened without his permanent scowl. She needed to get him to smile more often. It certainly would make him easier to be around.

Allie smiled back at him. "Being able to build your own home is a good skill to have." Realization dawned on her. "I guess that's why you decided to help me with the renovations… you have more experience than I do."

Bill put his hand on her lower back, just like he'd done in the diner. His touch made her stand up straighter, the sheer unexpectedness of it. Why did she like it so much? He guided her into the kitchen. There was barely enough room for them both, and once again Allie found herself in the position of being so physically close to Bill that their bodies kept touching accidentally, a brush here, a bump there.

He smelled of fresh hay, wood, and something indescribably masculine…perhaps that was just his natural musk. His body heat warmed her whenever her skin came within a few inches of him.

He swung the cabinet open, his bicep suddenly up right near her cheek.

"Mugs are up here," he said, "and dishes." He closed the cabinet and pointed to the sink. "Don't leave dirty dishes laying around—wash 'em as you go. I ain't cleanin' up after you."

Allie looked up at him in confusion. He'd been laughing with her only moments ago, and she'd even admitted that she understood why he was going to help her renovate the diner. So why was he being prickly again?

Maybe he was just trying to diffuse the tension… to remind them both not to get too friendly. Well, it was working.

"I know how to clean up after myself," she said.

"If you need to cook somethin', don't bang up my cabinets."

Allie shook her head. "You seem to have mistaken me for a bull in a china shop. However have I managed all this time without your micro-managing?"

"You think this is micro-managing? Wait till we get back to the diner," he warned, his face close to hers. "You'll have to earn my trust. You're gonna have to prove to me you're worth it."

"I am worth it," she said immediately.

"I bet," he murmured.

Any anger she had melted with those words. He didn't seem to be saying that sarcastically. His face was too close to hers to be anything but…sincere.

As if he realized just how close he'd gotten, Bill abruptly pulled back, knocking the back of his head on the cabinet behind him with a *thwack*.

"Oh no!" Allie gasped. "Are you okay?"

She reached her hand up to touch his head. Her fingertips grazed the ends of his dark hair, but Bill caught her wrist in his large hand.

"I'm fine," he said. Slowly, he let go of her wrist. "Are you okay? I didn't mean to grab you like that. It was just instinct or somethin'."

A look of genuine concern crossed his face, and he rubbed her wrist with his thumb.

"It's fine," she whispered.

"I um…" Bill shook his head as if to clear his thoughts. "Before the kitchen cabinet decided to attack me—"

"You can joke!" Allie interrupted, feigning shock. "The surprises just keep coming."

"You'll like this surprise, then," he said. "When you open the oven door, it won't go all the way."

Allie laughed and pulled the oven door open, to see. Sure enough, it only opened just enough that she'd be able to get something in and out, no more, before hitting the cabinet behind her.

"Just a suggestion," she said, "perhaps if you're going to help me with the renovations, we should spend a little extra time focusing on measurements."

She meant it as a lighthearted joke, but Bill shot her a warning look, as if she'd be sent to the principal's office if she kept it up.

And once again, his hand was on her back, the heat of it burning through the thin material of her blouse as he led her back out of the kitchen. She stumbled a bit on her heels. So dumb to wear heels to a ranch. What had she been thinking? This man obviously didn't care one bit about how she was dressed.

He walked her across the living room to the painted white door, and opened it. "You can stay in this room while you're here," he said.

Allie stepped inside the bedroom, looking around in surprise. The queen-sized bed was fitted with a rose floral comforter, and an iron bed frame. The dresser with the large mirror over it and the little accents around the room all spoke of a woman's touch. But there was nothing that spoke of Bill in this room.

"Where do you sleep?" Allie asked, suddenly unsure of herself. "I mean, I know you'll sleep at the apartment, but, where do you normally sleep and get dressed and everything? Here?"

It seemed like this room must've been Melody's. If it had been Melody's, didn't that mean it had been Bill's, as well? Was he giving up his bedroom for her?

Bill took off his hat and set it on top of the dresser by the door. "I'm not gonna bother you," he said, cocking his head. "You've made yourself clear enough. I'll be all the way at the end of the hall, in my room. They may call me Big Bad Bill, but I'll keep my hands to myself if it kills me."

If it kills me? Interesting…

"I didn't mean to offend you," she said. "That wasn't at all why I was asking where you normally sleep. I didn't think you were going to…barge in and ravish me or something." She forced a laugh and looked away, first at the bed, then the window.

Look at anything but the bed.

A strand of dark brown hair had fallen across Bill's forehead. "Right."

A flush heated Allie's cheeks, and she focused on not looking at either him or the bed—hard to do in a tiny room filled only with him, and a bed.

Now she was certain she was blushing. How ridiculous. It took a lot to make her blush—so how could this cowboy affect her like that?

"This looks like your wife's bedroom," she said finally. "And if it was Melody's bedroom, then I assumed it would be your bedroom, too. Since she was your wife and all."

"That's none of your business," he growled. "If you think you're gonna stay at my house, don't you dare talk about her."

He left her alone in the bedroom, her mouth hanging open like fish. Allie stormed after him and—though she had no idea what possessed her to do such a thing—grabbed his shoulder in an attempt to turn him around to face her.

Bill's body was immovable, a tree trunk against her palm. She wouldn't have been able to turn him if she had tried. But she got what she wanted anyway when Bill snapped his head back toward her and faced her full on.

"Is this what you want?" he growled, stepping in closer to her.

"You're tellin' me you ain't *done* with me yet?"

"Don't pull that 'my house, my rules' stuff," she said. "You're the one who sold me an uninhabitable apartment. It's your fault I'm here in the first place."

"And you're the one that showed up two weeks early."

"Forget it," she said.

He was right about that. And, she'd chosen to completely ignore everything he'd told her about needing to fix the apartment up first, because she'd thought it would be fine to rough it. Still, Bill needed to learn to talk to her nicely if they were going to be working together.

He couldn't just be mean one moment, and then sweet the next. There had to be an in-between. A cordial business-partner type of relationship.

"I'm too exhausted to fight," Allie said. It wasn't an apology or admission of being wrong, but it was her way of putting up a white flag, at least for now. "I think I need to take a nap and charge my phone before I can go back to start cleaning up the diner," she admitted. "Is that...okay?"

"Are you asking my permission to fall asleep?" The anger faded from his face, and he raised an eyebrow in amusement.

Allie laughed at the absurdity of it. "I guess I was," she said. "I thought you'd like that..." Ooh, that sounded a touch too flirty. She tamped it down a notch. "I need to get out of the heels."

Not much better. What was it about the heat of an argument that made Bill seem so...attractive to her? It must be his testosterone rising—she could sense it. Hormones, nothing more. She kicked off her heels right where she stood, and picked them up to bring into her room.

Bill looked at her. "Now you're even tinier," he mused. "You're gonna get a crick in your neck starin' up at me all the time like that, you know."

He was too handsome for his own good. Thank goodness he was a jerk as well—that made it easier not to want to mix business with dating. Though Allie couldn't ignore the tiny voice inside that suggested a few dates after the painful separation from her former husband would be nice. As long as she didn't let her heart get involved. And as long as they kept the business out of it.

No. Bill was clearly still tortured by memories of Melody. He probably had no desire to start up a "just dating for fun" sort of deal. But were they ever friends at all? Or had they gone from emailing about business to flirting online?

Stop that. No point in trying to reevaluate what she thought she knew about him. Now she had Bill in real life, and their relationship from now on was what was real.

She turned and walked into her room and shut the door. As long as she could actually sleep in this stranger's house (that's what he was, no need to think otherwise), in his dead wife's bed, then she'd be ready to tackle cleaning up the mess she could now proudly call fifty-percent her own. And no matter what, she absolutely wouldn't let herself dream about how amazing working with Bill would be, if only they could both avoid either killing each other, or falling for each other.

Either one seemed like a real possibility at this point.

* * *

Bill sat heavily on the couch in the living room, his hand automatically running across the cracks in the leather along the back. The leather was seriously beat up, with worn spots and scratches. The nice thing about it, though, was at least no one was afraid of messing it up. When the guys came 'round to visit and fill him in on the goings-on at the ranch, they were glad to have a place to kick up their boots after a long day on the mountain or working with the cattle.

It was a bit early in the season for the fireplace, but staring into the dancing flames always soothed his soul. It was better than TV (at least he thought so, but then again, he didn't have a TV). The only problem with sitting on his couch was the vantage point: looking straight at the room where Allie napped.

How many nights had he done the same thing, over two years ago? Just staring at that shut door, wishing his wife would come out and simply… sit on that busted couch with him. It wasn't fair to expect her to love him the way he did her—how do you match something so strong that the loss of it nearly killed him, even now?

Melody had never truly loved Bill, she'd even admitted it herself. They'd only dated briefly before he proposed, and she'd said yes because she wanted children before her clock ran out. It was only a few short months after their wedding that she'd had the first miscarriage. She was different after that, she pulled away, and any talk of their future together was gone. At least when they had the idea of a baby to keep them together, she'd been able to hold onto that hope that she might learn to love her husband. As for Bill, he'd fallen fast. She'd been so kind, so tall, so beautiful. And knowing that she had his child growing inside of her had made him fiercely protective of her.

It's not Melody in that room anyway. Forget about it.

No, it certainly wasn't Melody—silent, depressed Melody. She'd hated living on the ranch with him, hated collecting the eggs from the chickens, tending to the garden. She wouldn't go near even his most gentle horses. Zach, Eric, Jay, and Chris had done everything in their power to make her feel at home on the ranch as well, but nothing worked. She'd retreated further and further into her shell.

On the night she'd left him to go stay at her mother's house— even her own separate bedroom wasn't far enough from Bill for her—the fateful night she swerved in front of some poor trucker on his way home, and died. When Bill heard the devastating news, he'd wondered if she'd done it on purpose.

He still wondered.

Melody was the closest thing he'd had to a relationship with a woman that went beyond a few dates and a fling. But could it truly have been love when the other person didn't love you back?

It was strange to have another woman in the house, especially since Allie was the exact opposite of Melody. She was feisty and loud where Melody was not, even short when Melody was tall. Allie had verbally sparred him with such passion, but Melody had stopped even pretending to want or care about communicating with him, her own husband.

So he needed to stop looking at that door and imagining Melody was behind it.

Allie was her own woman—the kind of woman Bill had never imagined himself feeling attracted to, despite the fact that seeing her name in his inbox had been the highlight of his day for the past several months. Yet here he was, interrupting himself when he was with her just to look at her, to hear her shout or whisper or feel her brush up against him...

No, Allie was no longer just an unseen confidante, no longer solely the woman he'd befriended online sight-unseen. She was *here*, right behind that door, in person.

What would happen between them, now that their relationship had been brought into real life?

Chapter Seven

WHEN ALLIE WOKE up, it was to a rooster crow at dawn. She shot up in bed. What on earth had happened? She'd only meant to take a little nap.

That was a whole half-day wasted last night, when she could have been cleaning up the diner. Apparently, Bill had let her just sleep all the way through till morning. She must've really needed the sleep after all that driving, so it was probably a good thing.

And she wouldn't have wanted him waking her up, right? That would've involved him coming into her room while she slept, seeing her so vulnerable like that. She didn't want to be vulnerable in front of Bill. He needed to learn as fast as possible that having half-ownership with her meant she was also the boss. Not only him—in *addition* to him.

Two bosses…that could work, why not?

She peered her head out the guest room door, but didn't see him. The cabin was small enough that if he was there, she'd know.

"Bill? Are you here?" she called, just to be sure.

No reply. It was almost half past six in the morning. He was probably still sleeping at the apartment.

Allie grabbed her toiletry bag and went into the bathroom, with its river-rock floor and shower stall. No tub.

When she was all showered, dressed (sensibly this time, in jeans and a tank-top with a sweater for the early-morning chill), and ready to get to work, Allie walked down the driveway that would eventually lead her to the gravel road to the farmhouse.

It felt good to walk. In Miami, she'd been afraid of the very real threat of getting mugged... or worse. There had been too many stories on the news about crimes against early-morning female joggers (and in one recent instance, a woman just waiting for her bus). That and the sticky, humid heat of Florida had always kept Allie from exercising outdoors.

But here in Bear Creek Saddle, the air was crisp and smelled of cows, grass, and manure, (which wasn't nearly as disgusting as she'd have imagined it would be). Maybe she was just getting used to it? Either way, the walking helped clear her mind.

By the time she'd reached the farmhouse, that feeling of joy mixed with excitement and anticipation was bubbling up inside of her, making her cheeks warm and her vision extra sharp. Her diner was going to be incredible—finally they could get started fixing it up!

"Good mornin', Allie."

She turned at the voice and saw Bill, walking slowly in front of Pirate, leading his wild stallion that had nearly killed her the day before. Pirate had blinders on—hopefully that meant he couldn't see her and get spooked. They were behind a post-and-rail fence, but if Pirate decided to crash through it to escape, nothing would stop him. Just like that moose—Pirate had a lot of unbridled, pure power. He could do anything before Bill would be able to stop him.

Allie's stomach flipped at the thought.

"Good morning," she said. "Thanks for letting me sleep all

night—I needed it."

Pirate tried to look at her, but Bill gave him some big lumpy sugar cubes and kept him moving.

"I could tell," Bill said with a laugh. "By the time you went to lay down, I couldn't tell if you were going to kill me, kiss me, or collapse."

"It's like you read minds," she deadpanned. "Those were all options on the table, definitely."

The fact that he'd said that though… that meant he could see she'd been flirting with him. Accidentally. How embarrassing and horrible.

Or was it? He was laughing about it now, after all.

"When I'm super-tired, I get punch-drunk," she said, shrugging. "I say silly things, so please don't think I meant anything by it."

Bill offered more sugar to Pirate to keep him following his lead. It was a simple task, to walk around, but the trust involved was staggering. How long had he been working with Pirate?

"Don't worry about me," she offered. "I haven't killed a single person yet, and I haven't kissed a man since my husband ran off with his secretary."

He nodded in silent acknowledgement.

She flushed and covered her mouth with her hand. She hadn't meant to bring up all that about her ex again, and yet the words had just escaped her as if of their own accord.

"Forget I mentioned that," she mumbled.

It was embarrassing to talk about her former husband's infidelity. It made her feel like maybe it was her fault. That if she'd been a better wife, he never would have strayed in the first place. It was pointless to take his adultery on her own shoulders now. Not like it would change anything.

"Don't worry 'bout it," Bill said. "I know what it's like to have a long dry spell."

Allie laughed nervously. If there were a convenient cave to hide in, she'd like to find it.

But…it was kinda nice of him to ignore the gaping wound she'd re-opened when she mentioned her ex, and focus on her relatively benign admission that she hadn't exactly been on the dating scene, instead. Almost as if Bill was as ready to stay on good terms with her as she was with him.

Bill kept walking, slowly, the huge black horse like a chained giant behind him, able to break free of his bonds at any time, but choosing not to.

Why? Just for a lump of sugar?

"I told you yesterday that we couldn't start over," Bill said, not looking at her. He was focused on working with Pirate. "But you can forget I said that, too."

"Thank you," Allie said. Hope sprung inside her. "That means a lot."

Bill glanced over at her and tipped his hat in acknowledgement.

His black cowboy hat. The same hat that he'd left on her dresser top when he first showed her the room—the hat she'd fallen asleep staring at, thinking of him.

Wait a minute…

Allie took a deep breath. "You went into my room while I was sleeping."

Bill stopped, letting Pirate walk without him. While Pirate picked up the pace, getting some of his energy out, Bill walked over to the wooden fence.

"I didn't touch you," he said, taking off his hat and wiping his brow.

A lock of dark hair dropped into his gray eyes, and Allie had to fight the urge to smooth it away for him.

"But you looked at me. For how long? Did you watch me sleep?"

A muscle in Bill's jaw flexed. "I went in, grabbed my hat, and left to head to the apartment. I may have taken a peek at you, just to make sure you were still breathin', that's all."

"Why would you think I wouldn't be breathing?"

Bill shrugged. "Just a stupid habit from when I'd check on Melody, that's all. I'd poke my head in to check on her. I did the same to you by accident."

"Okay," Allie whispered. "I'm not mad. But…I'm not Melody."

Bill's gaze faltered. "Hang on."

He jumped up onto and then over the fence, landing at her feet. Still looking at her, he pulled out his phone.

"Zach, Pirate's done for the morning." Bill paused and held up his finger to Allie, as if to say, "*One sec.*"

Bill hung up and pocketed his cell. His long, muscular legs seemed to have grown right out of the earth, like he'd been working on that ranch for so long, he wouldn't know what else to do if he tried.

And yet now he was going to work side-by-side with her to get the diner open. Allie was the one with five years of experience both as a waitress and a manager. She should be the one in charge. But when he'd said they could start over, that probably didn't mean forgetting her admission that she had no clue how to renovate a building.

It was Bill who knew how to build houses by hand, how to raise barns and construct chicken coops, and repair everything on his sprawling ranch. She needed him.

They needed each other.

"I wanted to go to the diner and get to work," Allie said. "But I need access to the business checking account first." She held her breath, hoping she wouldn't have to pull out the big guns again— her wrath, and the contract—to get him to hand her his check book.

"Let's go," he said, "It's in my office in the farmhouse. I can fill you up while we're there, too."

"Fill me up?" A vision of him offering a spoonful of raisin oatmeal to her waiting lips flashed through her mind, and she shook her head to clear it. She was already full, so she shouldn't be thinking about more breakfast.

Yeah, breakfast. Right. Nothing at all to do with envisioning a handsome man being romantic with her. *Go away, imagination.* She had work to do.

"Your truck—I mean, car." Bill shook his head, but she could tell he was holding back a smile.

Lord, be with me today, and keep me focused. She needed all the help she could get.

* * *

They swung by the bank on their way to the diner. The bank was unlike any she'd ever been to in Miami. In Miami, the lines were long, and the experience rushed, impersonal. Here in Bear Creek Saddle, the small credit union had no lines at all. There was only two people working there.

Bill got Allie access to the checking account, and a debit card.

Then, right in front of her, he transferred all of the money that was in the account (except for a small percentage) out into another account—one she didn't have access to.

"Hey," Allie said. "What did you do that for?"

"I've never given you money before. You're still a stranger in that way. If you decide to fix being broke by running off with that card and emptying the bank account, at least now you'll only take me for a little bit, instead of everything I have for this diner."

Allie felt like she probably should be angry about that, but it made so much good business sense that she had to just nod.

"I won't run off with the money," she said. "But I can see why you'd want to arrange your finances that way. Hopefully, after a little while, you'll trust me enough to know I'm not planning to rob you blind."

She winked at him and he actually winked back.

Wow, that was incredibly fun. He was really good at winking at her. In his emails, he'd never used emoticons. But as she would read what he had to say, she always mentally inserted them on his behalf. Smiley face. Winky face. Frowny face.

It was so much better having the real thing right in front of her. Did he feel the same way?

At the diner, Bill walked ahead of her and unlocked the door.

"Close your eyes," he said.

"Oh no," Allie said. "Let me guess. Someone stole all the copper plumbing."

Bill laughed. "Not quite."

He came around behind her, and placed his large hand over her eyes, effectively blindfolding her with his hands. "I got a surprise for ya."

Bill walked behind her with one hand over her eyes, and the side of his body pressed against hers, guiding her to walk straight. Inside the diner, the scent of the outside had been replaced by that of…paint.

"It's not finished," he said, "but Zach an' the guys helped me out while you slept."

He dropped his hand, and Allie blinked.

"Wow," she breathed.

The diner had been cleaned! All the bits of plaster, dirt, and cigarette butts from on the floor were gone. The graffiti (even the nice one about *RIP Fred in HEAVEN!!!*) was painted over with primer. The dust sheets had all been taken off, and the tabletops polished to their original luster. The holes in the wall (from what, who could guess) had been plastered over and smoothed. An old pool table, with its ripped green felt and battered legs and missing balls, was pushed to the side, ready to be refurbished and put back in business.

This was incredible. It meant she didn't have to waste time cleaning the diner before renovating it. She was ready to go.

"I can't believe you did this all while I slept," she said. "Thank you. So much."

Bill shrugged modestly. "Wasn't just me. Zach, Eric, Jay, and Chris, they all helped. Zach Walker found he has another talent, polishin' wood furniture. If he ever decides not to be a rancher, he's got a job as a maid." Bill laughed, and Allie joined him.

"I'm going to have to bake everyone brownies as a thank you," Allie murmured.

Now that the place was clean, she could really see it better, and figure out how she was going to make this diner better than ever.

Slowly, she took her time walking the space; her shoes touched every inch of the floorboards.

This was really going to happen. Her dream come true. But they couldn't afford to rest on their laurels just yet. There was still a lot of work to be done.

"I want to put in a dance floor over there," Allie said, pointing to an open space toward the back of the diner, imagining it surrounded by tables. "And over here," she pointed, "an elevated platform—a stage, really, but a small one—so that we can have live music."

On future Wednesday nights, she could also envision herself standing on that little stage, mike in hand, announcing Bingo numbers.

"We don't do that in this diner." Bill frowned. "It ain't a nightclub. We're not Miami here."

"The very fact that you think some live music, a tiny dance floor, and Bingo will turn this diner into a Miami-style nightclub really speaks to how little you know about these things," she said. "You may be in charge of how to physically make this happen in this renovation, but let's use my experience working in restaurants, too."

"Bingo?" That was all Bill had to say to that.

"Wednesday nights," she confirmed. Maybe she'd forgotten to say that out loud before.

Bill paced the floor where she wanted to put in a dance floor, something varnished just enough to make dancing more fun, without being too slippery. Maybe they could do line-dancing on Friday nights!

"I know this diner used to be the dark, quiet kind," Allie said.

"But in order for it to really be profitable, I want to make it the kind of diner that people drive to from other towns, because it's so fun. There will be plenty of times during the afternoon, and things like that, where it'll be quiet. We'll have a big screen TV right there," Allie pointed to a spot above the counter on the wall. "On Saturdays we can have the game on, and everyone can meet up with their friends and have some nachos while they watch the game together. Make it a bigger TV than anyone has in their house!"

Bill stopped pacing. "I like that idea," he admitted. "But, I don't like the idea of changing what Uncle Freddy had. It's what people are expecting." He paused. "That's what *I* was expecting."

"I know," Allie said. "And I know this is not Miami."

She walked across the room and took his hand in hers to get him to stop walking, pacing, and hear her.

"We don't want it to be Miami," she assured him. His hand was so big compared to hers. She had to force herself not to look at their hands together. "We can have a diner that's different than what your uncle had, and still have everyone be happy. We won't have live music every night, that will be special for one night on the weekends."

"Guys don't need that."

"I want this diner to be a place that everyone likes going to," she said. "If it's just a good-ol'-boys club, where men go to get away from their wives, the women won't come. But if the women come, it becomes a *destination*. It becomes a fun place. And more men will come to the diner. Families, with kids, too."

Bill shook his head and crossed his arms, dropping his hand from hers. "I don't like it. I know what this diner was, Allie. I spent my high school years helping out Freddy in the kitchen when I wasn't doin' chores on the ranch. At the time I thought it was just extra pocket money, but now that he's gone…maybe I had that experience so I would know what this diner meant to him."

"To him, or…to you, as well?"

Bill shrugged. "Yeah, to me too. Just saying, it needs to stay the same."

He had been so smart and supportive in his emails with her before she actually showed up. Now that Allie was here, doing what she'd said she would, he was just getting in the way of her dream.

"I'm going to break it down for you, Bill," she said. "I understand how much that time with him meant to you. But—" She paused; took a break. "Your uncle's diner was not making enough money for him to live on, without his army pension."

"So what?" he asked. "That doesn't make the diner a bad place."

"Not at all," Allie agreed. "But that's only because the diner has so much potential, as long as we can get on the same page."

He leaned back against the mahogany counter-top and looked at her, as if to say "try me."

"You have income from Melody Ranch," Allie said. "But I don't. And since I'm getting half of the profits instead of all of them, if I keep the status quo we'll never get this diner running. We have to get it running, Bill."

"You're the only one besides me who cares 'bout the fate of this diner," he said quietly. "It's why I chose you."

"It's always been my dream to have my own restaurant," she admitted. "But a simple fact of life is that I'm going to need enough money to live on. History proves that the way this diner used to be… does not bring in enough money to live on. Not even if I had all the profits, and definitely not since I'll only have half of it. I know that's hard to hear," she said, trying to soften her tone. "Especially if you had wanted to bring the diner back exactly as it used to be."

She took both of Bill's hands in hers. "Please," she said, looking directly into his intense gray eyes. "Let me take charge of this. I know that I need you, because you're the experienced one when it comes to renovations and building. I am not experienced with that. But I have a dream for this diner. I've been thinking about it for a long time. Please... help me make it a reality."

Bill was silent, but she could see the gears turning in his mind. She waited, not saying a word, for him to process everything she'd said. It would be a big change, she knew, but sometimes change was the best way to go—the *only* way to go.

"Okay," Bill said softly. "We can try it your way, an' I'll help you build what you need. But if it don't work to bring in the money—"

"Then we'll reconvene to figure out a new plan," she finished for him.

In his eyes she saw begrudging acceptance. He nodded.

Yay!

She wrapped her arms around his neck in an exuberant hug. He held back for a moment, and then his arms were around her waist, returning the embrace with a strong squeeze.

"It may take a little time," Allie warned. "We'll have to get the word out about all the new event things—something like: two-dollar Tuesdays for kids to get cheap meals when their folks bring them in, Bingo on Wednesday nights, maybe open discussion on the mic on Thursdays, live music and dancing on Friday nights, and dancing to the country radio hits on Saturday nights. That's what

I'm thinking."

She popped up and down on her toes with excitement. Her once-wary business partner was even grinning at her.

"Don't forget the game on Saturdays afternoons," Bill said.

"Thank you, Bill," she said. "Thank you for actually listening, instead of just laying down the law."

She stood on her tip toes and gave him the smallest kiss, his sandpaper-scruff chafing her lips.

"I'm glad you're here," Bill said, and touched the spot on his jaw where she'd kissed him. "It's better than any email."

"We make a good team," she said. "It's going to be…amazing."

* * *

Bill could feel Allie's excitement in the air. It was contagious; her energy enveloped him like an embrace. He grinned at her.

"I suppose we could put signs up on the bulletin boards around town," he suggested. "Did you have a name all picked out already, or anythin' like that?"

"Not really…what was it called before?" The only signage out front said *Burgers—Hot Coffee—Pasta*. That wasn't exactly a name.

Bill laughed. "Ya know, I don't even know? Everyone just called it 'the diner' or 'Freddy's Diner'. Not like there were any others. Don't even know if it had an official name."

"Well, in honor of your uncle," she suggested, "and to keep the name recognition, we could call it Freddy's Diner. Everyone will automatically know where it is."

"Yeah. I like that." The warmth in eyes betrayed his gratitude at her suggestion. At least one thing about the diner would remain the same.

"Hey—we should take out an ad in the county newspaper!" Allie added. "And maybe make a small webpage for the diner, put the menu up, and our number, directions, the weekly calendar of events, that sort of thing. Shouldn't be hard for me to take care of."

He hadn't thought of that for some reason. "Good call. You're smart."

She gave him a look, as if she couldn't tell if he was making fun of her or not.

"I already knew that," he added. "From your emails. But I like seein' how your brain works in action."

Her blonde hair was still a bit disheveled from when he'd had his hand over her eyes. Carefully, he reached over and smoothed back an errant piece. Her hair smelled good, like some kind of flower, something he'd smelled before. Jasmine? Lavender?

How strange that this woman he'd been exchanging emails with for three months now was here, in person. And he'd never known what she looked like, never pictured her as this beautiful, smart woman all wrapped up in a tiny package.

Allie smiled. "Thank you."

Her top lip was a bit smaller than the bottom one. Every once in a while she'd pull out a lip balm and smear it on without a mirror. Cherry Chapstick. It made her lips look a bit pinker, a bit shinier—but still natural. Looked nice.

Forget it. Focusing on her choice of chapstick her was a bad idea—it would only lead to other thoughts involving her lips. They had a business to run together. Getting all tangled up in inappropriate thoughts could ruin their working relationship permanently. And that was the only sort of relationship he could ever have...business.

"You're beautiful, too," he told her, barely aware he was speaking out loud. *Man!* His words, the compliments, seemed to pour out of him no matter how hard he tried to remind himself not to give her—or himself—the wrong idea. "I don't know how to act 'round you."

A pretty blush colored Allie's cheeks. "Same as before, I guess. Before we ever saw each other."

"But it ain't the same," he said, "bein' with you here."

"I like when you're nice to me." She gave him a playful tap on the arm. "Sometimes it seems like you're just being ornery to keep me at arm's length."

"Yeah," he said. "That's clearly not workin'." He sighed. "I can be a bit harsh sometimes. I apologize."

He wrapped his arms around her, pulling her close to him. Was being with her the wrong idea, after all? Did it have to be? Her body was putty in his arms, so accepting. He hugged her, needing to put every ounce of emotion he had into that embrace. Allie rested her head against his shoulder, and it felt so perfect. So right. It was an embrace that said *You are beautiful*, and it was an embrace that said *I'm glad you're my partner*. It was an embrace that said *I can't do anything at this moment, other than wrap my arms around you.*

He pulled back from the hug just a little, and looked down at her wide, wondering eyes. What would she do if he tried to kiss her?

Wait. *Don't do this, not with her.*

Reality hit him. He would be in business with Allie Crawford for a long time. Getting intimate with her was not the best idea, no matter how much he wanted her. It would complicate things.

And being with her was dangerous. Very dangerous.

After what happened with Melody, Bill had long-vowed he

would never fall in love again.

Chapter Eight

THE FOLLOWING DAY, Allie left the diner in a huff. Bill was so hot and cold. One moment, he's ready to go, right on the same page with her. The next, he thinks she's being too radical. Seriously, were they really going to have a gravel parking lot for their customers, when they could just pave it over like a normal diner would have?

"Gravel ain't so bad," he'd kept saying.

More importantly, when would he let go of the reins a bit, and let her do the job she'd come here to do?

She drove back to Melody Ranch, and wandered over to the far hay fields, where the green John Deere tractor was at work. Looked like the guys were over there.

Zach turned off the engine on the tractor, and smiled warmly at Allie. "What's up?"

"Where's everyone?" she asked. "I wanted to thank you all."

She hefted a pitcher of homemade lemonade, condensation dripping on the outside, the ice cubes clinking, and gestured with her head to the stack of red Solo cups in the plastic bag hanging from her pinky finger.

For whatever reason, somehow she hadn't expected the rugged young cowboy to be using much in the way of technology out there in the middle of nowhere, but he pulled a smartphone out, his thumbs flying across the screen with well-practiced dexterity. Within a minute, Eric, Chris, and Jay hung onto the west fence. Chris's hair was wet, as if she'd interrupted a shower.

"Wow, you guys are fast," she laughed. "Now I know to yell 'fresh lemonade' instead of 'fire' in an emergency."

"Did you see your diner yet?" Zach asked, and jumped out of the tractor to join them by the fence.

Eric pushed Zach's shoulder playfully. "And if she hadn't?" Eric asked. "You would've ruined it."

Allie laughed with them. "I just got back from the diner. And I saw yesterday how awesome you guys fixed it up. It looks incredible."

She handed each of them a plastic cup from the package, and took one herself. "To new beginnings," she said as she poured everyone some lemonade, and they touched the rims of their drinks.

"To finally havin' a place to go after the sun sets," Zach added, and they toasted again.

"To havin' a woman around who can make Bill get off his behind," Chris said.

The guys made an "Ohhhh" sound, like Chris had said what the others had been thinking. They toasted again.

Allie grinned, wiping the cold lemonade from her lips with the back of her hand. Would it be inappropriate to give each of them a hug? *Nah.*

"Thank you so much for spending time cleaning for me the other night," she said, hugging each cowboy in turn.

Their bodies, strong from the intense labor required on the ranch, felt comforting and warm as they gave her a quick squeeze back. But they didn't incite the same flutter of excitement she felt when Bill came near her. There was just something about Bill. Something different.

"It must've taken you guys till dawn to clean that whole place up the way you did," Allie said.

Zach winked at her. "Nah. With the four of us plus Bill attackin' something, it gets done fast an' right. Glad we could help."

"Your first meal is on me when the diner opens," Allie said. "In fact, soon as we're ready, we'll have a practice run to make sure everything is running perfectly. I hope you'll be our first guests."

"Oh yeah?" Zach asked with interest as he climbed back up onto the tractor, balancing the cup between his denim-clad thighs. "Think you'll be able to get this thing pulled together, even with Big Bad Bill breathin' down your back?"

"Big Bad Bill isn't nearly as bad as he thinks he is," she said, and winked back.

Or was he?

* * *

Sunday was a welcome respite from the work. She drove to church with the ranch hands to save on gasoline—with Chris and Jay sitting in the back of Zach's pick-up truck, and her sandwiched between Eric and Jay in the front.

Bill didn't go with them.

"It ain't you," Zach answered her unasked question. "He stopped goin' after the accident," Zach said. "But he'll come around."

* * *

Allie went to the barn, carrying some carrots from Bill's

vegetable garden. It was pretty cool, digging into the earth and finding something she usually only found on her supermarket shelves in the produce aisle. Maybe she could learn how to garden, too.

It was still so weird to think about the fact that this was her life now. She lived here, in Idaho, of all places. There was no going back to Miami. No more beaches or humidity or traffic or high crime rate…no more crowds of people. There were definite benefits to being here.

And here, she'd have a chance to make a difference. Being the only diner in town created a responsibility, of sorts. She could single-handedly provide some entertainment for everyone. Maybe they should have a senior night, or a girls' night out, too... the possibilities were exciting.

She grinned. It had been just like this before she'd moved here, as well. She couldn't get her mind off of the diner, off of all the things she wanted to do with it. And why not? It was finally her turn to run a business, and to make a difference in people's lives. To make people happy, to bring them together. She was itching to get everything ready so she could open the joint and have a big party.

If only Bill wouldn't keep stepping on her toes. He didn't like her plans for surround-sound speakers, either. But if they were going to have dancing (and they *would* have dancing, despite how Bill balked at making her a dance floor), the music couldn't just come from a jukebox in the back, right?

Well. maybe it could. The main attraction was going to be good food, after all. If she gave a little, maybe he would too. Compromise.

She approached a gray mare that appeared very calm. "Hi there, sweetie," Allie said brightly. "Want a carrot?"

The mare sniffed it, chomped it up, and then nuzzled her nose against Allie's palm.

"Now you're my new best friend?" Allie laughed. "That was easy! I'll come by and see you later."

She moved on down the stalls, talking with the horses, stroking their faces and necks when they were comfortable with her, indulging them with some good scratching, too, like her old horse used to love.

At the far end of the barn, off by himself, was Pirate. The black stallion stood alone in his stall, asleep on his feet. At least he wasn't upset, like before. It seemed walking with Bill had done Pirate some good.

She looked at the last carrot in her hand warily. Should she risk giving it to Pirate? Or would he try to trample her to death again?

This time, Bill wasn't around to whisk Allie up onto his horse.

"Pirate," she whispered.

Either he ignored her, or he was still asleep.

"I don't want to wake you," she said. "I have a carrot here, if you're interested."

Pirate's eyes opened. He sniffed, his huge nostrils seeming to search for her hand.

"Okay," she said. Her hands shook as she carefully offered it to the horse. "Here you go."

Pirate munched the carrot from her, and looked at her expectantly, as if wanting more.

"You're like a different horse," Allie said. "Maybe you're starting to like it here?"

The horse stared at her. She didn't dare touch Pirate, unlike with the other horses.

"You like Bill, I think. He isn't that bad," she acquiesced. "At least he gives you sugar."

"Oh yeah?" a deep voice said from the barn door.

Allie whirled, embarrassed. Bill stood there, his tall, broad, muscular body silhouetted by the setting sun. He leaned against the doorframe, and tipped his black Stetson in greeting.

Allie blushed. If she walked toward the barn to leave, she may as well be heading straight up to him, since he was in the doorway. She couldn't continue feeling annoyed at him, not with that cute smile on his face.

Allie meandered toward him, pretending she was aiming for the door, but he blocked her path just as she had blocked his at the diner.

"Do you really want to leave?" he asked, his voice low. He wrapped his arms around her waist, drawing her near. "I can't get you out of my mind."

"I don't have to leave," she whispered, tilting her head up toward his handsome face.

He gazed at her, her face reflecting back in his steel gray eyes.

Then—just as quickly as he'd done the first time they met, Bill gathered her up in his arms, holding her against his chest like a man carrying a bride over the threshold.

Allie squealed in surprise and delight, because this time she knew exactly who was holding her.

"What's going on?" she asked. She grabbed on around his neck to get a better hold, but he was so strong, there was no way he'd ever drop her. "Where are you taking me?"

"Hay loft," he said. "Though I gotta say, Zach an' the guys did more to bring in this year's hay than I did."

He carried her past the horses, to a tall wooden ladder secured at the base and top, leading nearly straight up to what was literally, just a loft with hay on it.

"That's a really great hay loft," she said politely, with a laugh. "I guess I never thought about how much hay you guys actually need to grow and harvest, and store."

"Let's go up an' talk more about hay." Bill smiled, a twinkle in his eyes. "Since you're so interested."

"You're flirting with me."

"Yes, ma'am," he agreed.

"But you were being such a jerk before."

"So I been told." Bill grinned at her, holding her against his chest as if she weighed nothing at all.

Allie had to laugh. Yeah, he was a jerk, but he was…Bill. And she couldn't get her mind off of him, either.

Allie stared from the bottom of the ladder all the way up. She grabbed hold of a rung, shook it hard, and it didn't budge. So it was sturdy, at least. Still, it was so high up.

"Think you can climb up there?" he asked, and set her on her feet.

"I'm scared to go up there with you," she admitted. She felt even shorter than before now that Bill wasn't holding her up. "We may just have to appreciate your hay from down here on the ground."

Bill frowned and wrapped his arm around her in a comforting embrace. "Are you scared to go up there with me," he asked, "or, are you scared to go up there, period?"

Allie laughed. "I think I can handle you," she said. "I'm not so sure I can handle climbing up the ladder."

"No problem," Bill said.

He lifted her up from the waist and pressed her torso against his, her legs dangling a good foot off the ground. She wrapped her legs around his waist tightly, with her arms around his neck.

"Close your eyes," he said. "I've got you."

Allie had never put her physical safety into someone else's hands before, not since she was a child. But for some reason, she trusted Bill completely—not just his physical strength, but his desire to keep her safe. She shut her eyes and nuzzled her face against his neck.

She wasn't going to look down.

Bill started climbing, but all she knew was what she could feel—the movement of his shoulders and thighs as he moved. With her eyes tightly shut, she could pretend they weren't fifteen feet off the ground.

Suddenly, Allie felt herself being gently pried off and set down on the scratchy surface of a hay bale. She opened her eyes.

The hay loft was huge, the square footage of the entire barn downstairs but with no partitions, and stacked from the back of the loft going forward with large wrapped cubes of hay—bales. Well, they were more rectangular-ish than square. Cuboid bales?

Doesn't matter. What mattered was she had made it up alive... and she was there all alone, with Bill.

In the front, where they sat, there was an open bale, with loose hay cushioning the wooden floor of the loft.

"That ride up wasn't as terrifying as I thought it would be," Allie said. Her pulse had begun to slow a bit, back to normal. She looked around the loose hay. "Why is this bale broken?"

Bill picked up some straws of hay and let them fall back onto the loft. "Easy access. Right now we've still got grass, though the morning frosts are comin' quick. The cows and horses are pretty happy."

"You've been saying that you haven't been doing much work on your ranch," she said carefully, not wanting to offend. "Why do you think that is?"

Bills sat on the wood, his knees bent in front of him, and rubbed something from the toe of his boot.

"Bein' a cattle rancher used to be my whole life," he said. "After Melody died... I didn't do anythin' that first year."

Allie put her hand on his shoulder. Having her husband leave her hasn't been the same, but she'd felt the same way after he was gone. An empty house, an extra empty pillow in bed...

While she couldn't know what he'd felt, she couldn't even imagine how much more suffering he'd gone through. It made her want to comfort him, to wrap her arms around him. To heal his tortured soul, just by giving herself to him, by showing him the love that he'd lost.

"It took a while... but I'm doin' better," he said. "Gettin' out more this past year."

"That's great. Time heals all wounds, at least that's what they say."

Bill shook his head, as if he didn't subscribe to the idea of time healing his wounds.

"Was...was Melody a believer?" she asked. Maybe she shouldn't have. Bill's eyes turned stormy at her question.

"I think so, yeah," he said, his voice thick. "She went to church every Sunday. Said grace. I even used to go with her. Not anymore."

He shook his head and cleared his throat, as if it had gotten too tight for comfort. "Ain't no point."

"No point in going to church?" she asked. "Because she wasn't there with you?"

"Nah—I just...I ain't exactly on talkin' terms with God these days. Not after Melody died."

Allie paused. She didn't want to say the wrong thing. Bill was finally talking to her, really talking, and what if she sounded preachy or pushy to him? *Give me the words to say, Lord.*

"Maybe..." She took a breath. While she hadn't been widowed, losing her husband against her will had put her through the ringer as well. "I'd understand if you were angry with God," she finally conceded. "I mean... we can't possibly know His plans, or see how He'll ever be able to work what happens for our good, or even how He'll get us through it."

"I'm not angry at God," Bill said softly. He winced. "I was, but that ain't it, don't you get it? I failed Him. I failed *her*. If I had been a better man, a better Christian, a better husband...none of this would have happened."

So he blamed himself for her death. "That must be such a heavy burden for you to bear," she whispered. "If that's how you feel."

"Yeah, well, that's how it is," he said. "Can't go back in time." His demeanor changed slightly, as if the subject of Melody was closed. "Heavy burden, as you put it—I didn't want to get out of bed, much less work or go to church. I was pretty much jus'...done."

"What got you out of your rut, then?"

He thought about it. "Emailin' with you, I guess."

"Really?" *Thank you, God, for working through me to help him where I could.*

Bill nodded, and shrugged, as if it wasn't a big deal. But it was. "You were excited. And you kept askin' me things, and askin' about the town. Having you there, on the other side of the country, pingin' my inbox every day…" He paused. "It's dumb."

"No it's not," she whispered.

"It just… it made me feel needed. Like I had someone holdin' me accountable. I had to answer you, tell you stuff." He peered into her face. "I should've told you more what to expect with the place. I'm a louse for makin' you feel betrayed."

Allie leaned over and hugged him. "Don't say that," she said, squeezing him fiercely. "It turned out for the best. Everything's moving along great."

He kissed her cheek, pressed against his own, before she let go of him. The gesture was sweet, but it also served to remind her how close they were. Physically close, yes. But he'd also told her more just now than he had since she'd gotten there. It was as if all the intimacy they'd built up from their beginnings online had finally crystallized in him as real.

They were real. Whatever this relationship was, it existed here, right here in Idaho, and not just online.

"I been thinkin' about selling Melody Ranch to the guys," Bill said. "Zach an' them should own this place."

Allie gasped at the revelation. "I don't know what to say to that," she said. "Wow."

"I'm ready to move forward. Too many bad memories in my house, on the ranch. I can't shake 'em."

"I think it's a good idea, I guess," Allie said. "Especially if you feel like you need a fresh start. The guys seemed to have everything handled here. But this was your father's cattle ranch, and your grandpa's too, if I remember correctly."

He nodded that she was right. "I've forgotten all the things I've already told you."

"Are you worried about giving that legacy up?"

"Well, I'd already renamed it when Melody moved in," he said. "I shouldn'ta done that."

Bill took her hand and pulled her over next to him, leaning up against a bale of hay. He wrapped his arm around her, and pulled her close to him. "I think I want you near me so much 'cause before we met in person, our emails made me feel close to you... But I could never see you or touch you. Now I can, an' I'm takin' advantage of that."

Allie shook her head and smiled. "If I'm enjoying your company, then you're not really taking advantage." A short, nervous laugh escaped her lips. "As long as you don't, you know, take advantage for real."

"I'd never."

The conversation stilled. The only sounds were of the horses shuffling below, and of their own breathing.

Bill brought his hand to her belly, and slowly moved over her shirt to her waist, his hands roving gently as they sat there. Down her arms, to her hands, drawing a lazy circle on her palm.

Yes.

"I ain't married," Bill said softly. "Not anymore. And I don't have a kid to pass Melody Ranch on to. There's no reason for me to stay on at the ranch."

Allie nodded, hearing him, but also *feeling* him, the slow, steady pressure of his hands as he spoke. He touched her fingers, caressing them.

She inhaled, thrilled—and a bit surprised—by the intimacy. It was something that was meant to happen, she knew. Every interaction they'd had, had led up to this very point in time.

Bill smiled at her reaction. "Besides, if I'm workin' at the diner with you—that's the family business too. At least now I'm actually doin' something with it."

He brought his hand all the way up her arm to her face, her cheek, and held her there. His callused palm against her sensitive skin made her dizzy with need.

"I haven't been this excited about someone—I mean, some*thing*... in a long time. Gettin' the diner open again," he said. "It's gonna be big."

Allie looked up at him through heavy lidded eyes. "You didn't carry me up here to actually show me the hayloft."

"No," Bill said. He took his hat off, and dropped his lips to hers. "I didn't bring you up here jus' to show you the hay."

Her breath caught even as reality rushed at her. "I can't have s—"

"—just a kiss," he promised, "that's all I ask."

Chapter Nine

EVERY REASON WHY they shouldn't be doing this flashed through Allie's mind simultaneously. Bill was going to be her business partner, and mixing business with pleasure was a bad idea. She still had a broken heart from losing her husband. It had been a year, but Bill would be the very first man that she'd kissed since the annulment.

She was afraid of getting her heart broken again. He probably didn't even know how much power he had. He could crush her heart if she wasn't careful, if she didn't leave up some sort of wall.

Those hands, that mouth of his, on her lips, her neck… He brushed his lips across her cheek. The stubble on his jaw scratched at her sensitive skin, and she relished every sensation.

"You are beautiful," Bill said.

"You're beautiful, too," Allie said. It was the truth.

Her stomach fluttered with excitement. *This is happening.* For the first time in a very long time, she was letting herself experience romance with someone other than her ex.

The emotion in his eyes heated her very soul.

As frightened as she'd been at the idea of climbing that ladder, she'd known she could trust him with her physical safety. She could trust him to take care of her. Bill had earned that. It was a good feeling to have.

"I don't know what doin' this means," Bill said. "Kissing you...I don't want to lead you on."

"After my last relationship," she said, "I have good reason not to make the same mistake again. Just stay honest with me."

Bill nodded. "Same," he said, his voice raw. "'Long as we're on the same page."

"We are."

They didn't move, holding each other tight.

Allie's body trembled. "We shouldn't start something we can't finish. I can't—"

"I know," he said. Bill paused. "I waited till I was married, too. And I'll wait again."

What did that mean? Did he see himself getting married again someday?

Did he see himself getting married...to her?

"But just a kiss doesn't feel wrong, does it?" he asked.

"As long as we stop at that," she whispered.

"This is the first time thinking romantically about a woman doesn't feel like I'm... betrayin' her."

"You're my first, too." The first man other than her husband she'd kissed, or even looked at twice, since he'd left her. And no, it's didn't feel like a betrayal. It felt...right.

Allie gripped his hand in hers, and they sat in silence.

Please, God... Don't let me fall in love with Bill.

I can't go through it again.

Chapter Ten

"HEY, GINGER!" ALLIE called as she entered Ginger's General Store, the bell on the doorframe jingling. The homey scent of candles and pies greeted her.

"Oh good! I need more flyers," the woman said, wiping her hands on the lower half of her shirt as she came out from behind the register. "I been puttin' one in almost every bag when folks come in!"

"Wow," Allie said. "That's awesome. Thank you so much for supporting me…us. The diner."

"All of you," Ginger agreed, nodding. "And you're very welcome, hon. I'm just happy to have a place to eat out, right here in town! No more drivin' an hour each way. I can't stand driving in the city, it's awful."

Allie laughed. The nearest city had about 45,000 people in it, but quite a few dining options since it was right off the freeway. Truckers often stopped for a meal or to sleep in the motel when they traveled through.

"You probably won't want to move to Miami," Allie suggested.

The new stack of flyers for the grand opening party of Freddy's Diner had events listed on it (Bingo night!), and even a black and white photo of herself. That had been Bill's idea, so that when folks saw her they'd know who she was.

"I'd melt in Florida," Ginger said. "Have you found live music yet?"

"No," Allie said. "Why? Do you know someone?"

"No," she laughed, as if the idea of her knowing a musician was preposterous. "But everything else's lookin' ready to start, for the date on the flyer?"

"We're working on it," Allie said. "I mean…yes. The diner will be ready." If only she felt as confident as her words. There was still so much to do. "If I have to go without sleep from now until the grand opening, the diner *will* be ready."

From her mouth to God's ears, as her mother would say. Hopefully.

"That's the spirit, hon! So have ya had to call in the boys on the ranch for backup from Big Bad Bill yet?"

"Nope." Allie grinned and shook her head. "Thanks for handing out the flyers, Ginger. You rock."

As Allie left the store, the bell on the top of the door frame ringing to announce her exit, Ginger called, "Keep your chin up and don't let him scare ya!"

Right. She wouldn't let Big Bad Bill—or the tenuous thread their relationship balanced on—scare her.

Chin up.

* * *

Renovations at the diner were going well. The afternoon sun filtered through the new windows along the wall, and Allie squinted, trying to reduce the glare. Maybe some blinds were in order? Bill had already laid about half of the new black and white checkered tile floor, and it was looking really good.

Allie had painted two of the walls green, to complement the evergreens outside. Paint roller in hand, she stared at the area behind the counter. Should that be green too? Or did she need an accent color?

"What do you think, Bill?" she called.

Bill glanced up from laying tile with a sigh and looked at her quizzically. He acted like she'd been asking his advice on everything... oh, wait. She actually had been. Why not? That big, bad cowboy had more of a knack for interior design than he gave himself credit for.

"Should we do a different color for the wall behind the register counter?" Allie pressed. "Some sort of bold accent color?"

"I dunno. You can figure it out." He paused, cocking his head as he observed the room. "Mix it up."

"Definitely."

She wouldn't point out that he had just spoken more words to her than he had all day combined. *Way to make a woman feel awkward after kissing her, dude*, she mentally scolded him. But not out loud. Bill would come around.

Red would look too Christmas-y with the green. Besides, she didn't want to give the place a fast-food feel. And the color couldn't be too girly... or could it? Would guys come to eat in a pink diner? Allie laughed to herself at the mental image of a crew of tough cowboys hanging around a bubble-gum pink counter. *Nice.*

Wait a minute...

"Dark blue!" she exclaimed. "And I'll string little pinpoint lights all over it. It will look like a starry night!"

From the corner of the diner, Bill set the last tiles he'd cut to size, set down his tools, and brushed his hands off on his jeans. He walked over and stood next to her, his arms crossed against his chest, and stared at the wall with renewed appreciation.

"Never would've thought of that," he said. "But I like it."

"Thanks," Allie said. She had to run to the paint store now.

As she turned to go, Bill grabbed her wrist. She gasped and stopped in her tracks.

"Wait," he said, holding her in place to keep her from leaving.

Allie looked at him warily. "Okay…I'm waiting."

"I ignored you this mornin' when I came back to the house. Wasn't intentional… I just didn't know what to say."

"'Good morning' would have been appropriate," she suggested. She smiled to soften her words. "Look, I get it. You don't want to make this—us—into a 'thing'. Neither do I. I'll probably be single for the rest of my life, if I've learned anything after my shamble of a marriage."

Bill shook his head and touched her shoulder, letting his hand linger for a moment before dropping it back to his side. She immediately wanted it back, the comforting weight of his hand.

"I don't know what to say around you," he admitted, "and I'm scared as all-get-out to start somethin' new, too."

"Then what are we doing here?" Allie asked.

She winced at how harsh the words came out. The last thing she wanted to do was push him away. And yet, keeping a protective wall between them seemed like the easy way out. It was so natural, so instinctive to keep him at arms' length. His painfully clear unease with their growing feelings made is so easy for her to keep that distance, too.

But she wanted to embrace him. Even more, she wanted him

to need her, not just as a business partner, or as a girl to kiss in the hayloft, but as… what? A girlfriend? Wife?

Why? Where would that even lead? It was the wrong road to go down. Allie had already been down that road once before, and look how that had turned out. She'd given her entire life to a man and promised him "till death do us part"—but her ex couldn't even keep his vows for a few months.

Would Bill be any different?

Maybe it was her own fault. The one common denominator in any relationship she'd ever had, obviously, was herself. If none of her relationships lasted, including the one where she actually got *married*—and then that didn't last either—why would it ever be different with Bill Edwards?

"We should keep things professional," Allie said. "Because if we keep this up, if we keep…" She paused, unable to find a word for what they were doing. "One of us is going to get attached, and it'll probably be me. I can't afford to have my heart stomped on again. And I refuse to ruin my new business because of a man."

Bill jerked back as if she'd slapped him, his expression pained.

"'Suppose you're right," he said. He looked away from her, back to the wall, as if envisioning it again with blue paint. "I can't stop thinkin' 'bout you, thinkin' 'bout the hayloft, too. But, if I keep thinkin' like that…"

"What?" she asked, crossing her arms protectively in front of her chest. "If you keep thinking of me like that, then what?"

"Come on, Allie," he said, his gaze snapping back to hers. "Don't push me."

She waited. She wouldn't let him bait her into a fight just to distract from an important conversation.

"I have feelings, too," he said quietly. "You're not the only one who could get all attached if we keep on like this." His voice cracked with emotion. "I'm still broke in half from Melody dyin'."

He left her standing there, and walked back over to where he'd left his tools, picking up a piece of extra tile on his way.

"If I fell in love with you—man, if I lost you too…" Bill wasn't looking at her anymore, instead staring intently on the partially-constructed platform in front of him. "There would be nothin' of me left."

He said the last words so softly, she almost wasn't sure if she'd heard them correctly or not. The sorrow in his voice…she'd never want to be the cause of that pain.

You'd still have God. But she didn't say it out loud. Up in the hayloft, when everything was quiet and intimate, talking about Jesus with him felt natural. Was she so scared of frightening him off now, by laying a little truth down on him?

The moment passed.

"I'm going to go out and buy blue paint and some little white lights," Allie said tonelessly. What else could she say? No one could bear the burden of being the woman who'd completely broken a strong man, who'd killed his very spirit.

It wouldn't be her. Not today, not ever. Bill was better off without her… he'd said as much, and knowing him—knowing how deeply, how passionately he could feel—she believed him.

She tried to force every warm thought about Bill Edwards out of her mind, so she could focus on work. Focus on the renovation.

Lord, help me forget him.

Bill was just her business partner, and it was better that way.

"Don't forget to look at the measurements I drew up for that platform stage," Allie added, and shut the door behind her.

She didn't mean for it to slam. But it did.

* * *

The steam from Allie's shower fogged up the large mirror in Bill's bathroom. She ran the water cold, and grabbed her purple toothbrush, pausing for only a moment when it grazed against Bill's green one. How perfect their toothbrushes looked together in the holder. Like they were meant to be, their handles touching as if they were as drawn to each other as much as their owners were.

It had been nine days since renovations had begun, and amazingly, things were already taking shape. The new checkered floor tiles were all grouted in, and the little stage platform was ready in the back. The new paint and lights and booths along the walls looked amazing, and the chairs left over from Uncle Fred had been re-varnished in black for a sleek look. They looked amazing with their recently-acquired tables and the booths Bill had installed. All she needed now was to make their first purchase of food to stock the pantries and large, shiny stainless-steel refrigerators Bill had his buddy refurbish.

Allie finished brushing her teeth, and stared at herself in the mirror. The dark circles under her eyes displayed her exhaustion to anyone who saw her.

"Zombie," she murmured to herself as she dabbed a bit of concealer on, blending it until she almost looked rested—or at least less like the walking dead.

She and Bill had been working together around-the-clock to get this done. Fixing her apartment was on hold until the diner was open, per her own request. She needed the money the business would bring in.

And maybe, just maybe, she didn't want to move out of Bill's house. Despite everything. Despite needing to distance herself…there was comfort in knowing he was right there, near her during the day. And he seemed perfectly fine with leaving every night to sleep at the apartment, and coming home the next morning to head for the shower and then the kitchen for breakfast.

They worked really well together, and he'd been friendly to her. But he hadn't touched her, not even once. It seemed as if he'd had to stop himself, sometimes, from small gestures such as touching her shoulder to get her attention.

But she *missed* his touch. It was good that they had their moment in the loft, perhaps, but all it had served to do was to show her exactly what she was missing.

Allie pulled on a pair of comfy work jeans and a casual sweatshirt, and opened the bathroom door—

The door hit something and bounced back at her. She shrieked with surprise.

"Whoa!" Bill said, rubbing his forehead.

He was dressed…or rather, um, *undressed*, for the shower, with a towel wrapped around his narrow waist like a kilt.

"I'm so sorry!" Allie said. "Did I hurt you?" That *whack* sure sounded like it had to hurt.

Don't look at him. Don't think any thoughts.

She looked down. Focused on his bare feet, big and callused. No, that's not good. She shifted her gaze to the bath rug. Away from all the muscles and the towel.

"I deserved it," Bill joked. "For makin' you blush like a school girl."

She huffed. Not like she had never seen a man without a shirt on before. She'd been *married*, for goodness sake. But Bill was right—her face burned.

"I'm sorry," he said quickly, "I shouldn't be…uh…"

Flirting? Half-naked? Standing in the doorway, so she couldn't run past him with as much dignity as she could muster?

Bill laughed as if to fill the awkward silence. "Must've been the knock on the head."

He moved his hand from his forehead, and Allie risked a glance up. His forehead wasn't as red or painful-looking as Allie had feared, thank God. No big bump or anything.

Look away now. No need to see any part of him other than the one spot she'd whacked with a door.

He cleared his throat uncomfortably.

"Bathroom's all yours," she murmured.

They swept past each other in the doorway, each looking away in embarrassment.

"Sorry 'bout that—I wasn't thinkin'," he said as he closed the door behind him.

Well, it *was* his house. She was usually already done with the shower and drying her hair in the guest room by the time he came back from the apartment and needed the bathroom for himself, but she'd slept in a bit. Wasn't his fault she caught him in a state of undress. Or was it?

Allie shook her head and sat on her bed—Melody's bed.

What were Allie and Bill really trying to accomplish with these moments…passing in the hall or the kitchen, unable to give in to temptation, but letting themselves be tempted anyway? Their desire was not just for physical contact, but for each other. At least it was that way for her.

What did any of this mean?

Bill had said that he didn't want to get involved in a relationship. He had said he would never love anyone again.

He wasn't doing much to indicate he could be changing his mind—other than flirting with her. And talking with her like they used to, when all they could see of one another was the words in an email. And God help her, she liked it. A lot.

Was she just setting herself up for the one thing she'd sworn she'd never let happen again—complete, and utter heartbreak?

Chapter Eleven

THAT SUNDAY IN church, Allie sat in the middle of the wooden bench, with the guys from the ranch seated—or rather, sprawled, with their long legs and muddy boots—next to her.

As they sang along to *Amazing Grace*, the big double door in the back of the church opened, letting in a whoosh of air.

"Well, I'll be," Zach whispered, craning his neck. "God *does* answer prayers."

Allie turned to look. It was Bill.

Her smile widened and she waved him over to their pew, but Bill just tipped his hat to her as he took it off, and sat on one of the folding chairs against the back wall.

Lord, please let Bill hear what You need him to hear. And...thank You.

She sat back against the hard, polished wood, her smile still stretched from ear to ear.

* * *

The following week when Allie hit the switches from behind the granite countertop at Freddy's, the overhead lights in the room darkened as the space lit up with ambient lighting. The little pinpoints of brightness, the stars that sparkled on the wall behind her, gave the space a distinctly special feel. Two TV monitors in the corners of the wall behind the diner were off, for now, but the first weekend after opening they would start showing whatever big game was playing. The pool table, the same one that had been in complete disrepair not too long ago, looked brand-new after getting refurbished. A new pool set, balls, and pointers hung neatly on a rack on the freshly-painted wall.

"This is our diner," Allie whispered in disbelief. "I am an actual co-owner of a business I'm super excited about."

Bill stood behind the gleaming countertop with her, gracing her with the biggest smile, all straight white teeth.

"Yeah, you are," he said. "You're gonna be great at running this place. Folks 'round here, they see you. They see you workin' hard, building something for the good of the town."

"You really think I'll fit in?" Allie asked. "I've been warned about how hard it is to fit in and feel welcomed in such a small town. Not that I've found that in Bear Creek Saddle," she added quickly. "I've just been too busy here—with you—to meet with people outside of church."

"You'll make friends real quick," Bill said, with the certainty of a man who could tell the future. "Especially after the official opening night."

She smiled. "Thanks for agreeing to cook—"

"—only until you get someone better than me," he broke in to remind her. "I'm not a fancy chef. All I know is what my pop taught me."

"Having a grandfather who ran the mess hall in the army is more than most guys can say, cooking-wise."

"He taught me everything he knew," Bill agreed, "but I was still young when he died. Twenty-five and busy with the ranch at the same time."

"We just need a guy who knows his way around a grill and how to work fast," she said pointedly. "You'll be fine and you know it. Your Pop would be proud."

"Pop and Uncle Freddy were brothers…I wish they could see this place now." His forehead and cheeks reddened.

Was he blushing? This was important to him—more important than he'd been letting on.

With the renovations complete and the food stocked, the place was ready to go. They only needed one thing: a "practice night" to work out any bugs before the Grand Opening party.

"Place looks good," Bill said, whistling under his breath as he took it all in. "*You're* good. This never would've happened without you."

"God is good. But thank you for saying that," Allie whispered. She stepped back slowly with a smile. "You did an amazing job yourself, you know. I was lucky to have such a skilled jack-of-all-trades."

The gravel crunched in the parking lot outside. Allie, in the spirit of choosing her battles, had let Bill win when it came to not paving over the lot.

"They're pulling up," Bill said. "The guys'll love this. Usually, they just bring a radio and some buddies to tailgate outside of the barn," he said with a laugh. "An' annoy the horses."

Well, at least the new diner could top a barn, right? It would be pretty embarrassing to be outranked by a farm structure as the best place in town for fun.

The main door opened, and Zach strolled in, followed by Eric, who wore a sleek cowboy hat Allie could only assume was his "clean" one, or his "dress" cowboy hat, unlike the battered hat he wore on the ranch. Jay and Chris followed, their hair still wet from showering after a hard day's work.

"Welcome to Freddy's Diner," Allie said. "You guys are the first to see it like this."

"Wow," Zach exclaimed the moment he entered. "And great name. Real good."

He ran up to the diner and high-fived Bill, and then for good measure, Allie as well. Allie laughed and slapped his hand back with exuberance. Now her palm stung, but she didn't mind. A stinging palm sometimes feels like victory. Tonight was important.

The other guys walked around, checking everything out.

"I can't believe this is the same diner," Zach said. "You did a real good job, Allie."

"Thanks!" she said. "Bill did, too."

The guys laughed. Jay said, "Bill's put in more man-hours on this diner then he has on th—"

Chris jabbed Jay in the chest, interrupting him.

"Oww," Jay muttered.

Bill pulled his black Stetson down over his forehead and shrugged. "What can I say? Allie motivated me to want to come to work."

"I'm gonna have to wear a skirt to get 'im back on the ranch," Eric joked, "I know it."

"Would you at least shave your legs first, or is that asking too much?" Bill deadpanned, and the guys cracked up laughing.

Allie could already imagine what they'd start daring each other to do if she let this go on. Might be interesting, but they had a job (albeit a very enjoyable one) to do.

"Okay everyone," Allie said quickly, "food is on the house tonight. We'll need to try some different dishes, try some fountain drinks, check out the sound system, the dance floor, the stage... I want to sit in every chair and booth in this place, and make sure that everything is in working order and ready for customers."

The guys agreed heartily. That was definitely something they were up for helping with. What could beat free food in exchange for being "practice" customers?

Bill gave them a quick salute as he opened the swinging kitchen door. "Now the real test begins. Pray for me."

He said it like he might be half-joking, but Allie caught Zach's eye and knew they both had one thought, simultaneously: *Lord, please be with Bill.*

After that brief moment, Allie shook her head to clear her thoughts. "Alright, my friends—would you like a booth for four?"

"Yes, please," Zach said. "Let's see if these booths can really hold four guys without us having to sit on each other's laps."

Allie took their orders, playing waitress—the one role she knew like the back of her hand—until she could hire a couple of teenagers to help her out. Running the business-end of the restaurant and being the hostess would probably end up being her full-time position once she got some help. If they were busy enough to afford the help, that was.

When Jay tried to order "the same" as the bacon cheeseburger with fries that Eric ordered, Allie raised her eyebrows pointedly till he ordered something different, with different sides and everything. They needed to test whether this would *really* work with Bill at the grill in back.

Later in the evening, with everyone stuffed to the gills, it was clear: Yes. This really worked. Bill was fast and accurate in the kitchen. His grandfather had taught him well, and the lessons Bill had learned as a teen working with his great-uncle Freddy in the old diner's kitchen had stuck.

They all stood and applauded when Bill came out of the back kitchen, his white apron draped over one broad shoulder.

"Don't clap," he said, biting back a laugh as he shook his head. "Wasn't nothin' big."

"It was good food and you did a good job," Allie replied simply. Knowing Bill as she did now, he'd take those few words to heart more readily than any flowery endorsement she could truthfully give him.

Bill joined the guys as they tried out each chair, each seat in the place, and fixed a light fixture that shone too brightly in their eyes in one area, until it was perfect. Their practice night was going better than she could have imagined it.

Allie left her position behind the diner, and stood behind Bill, waiting for her turn to play pool. It wasn't a bad situation, getting to watch the five handsome, strong men work the pool table, their deep, baritone voices mingling as they talked and laughed.

"You guys could've brought your girlfriends," Allie said, "to balance out all this testosterone."

"We'll bring dates for opening night," Chris said.

Zach shrugged noncommittally from his chair, a lock of his light brown hair falling over his forehead. "I'm still looking for a girl." He kicked his boots up onto a table.

Bill glared at him.

"They're not *that* dirty," Zach protested, but he dropped his boots to the floor instantly.

In moments like that, Allie could almost imagine what it had been like when Zach and the guys first starting working for Bill when they were teenagers, and Bill was at the "advanced age" of his mid-twenties.

"I have to admit, it's hard to believe that hard-working, good guys like you four aren't already taken." Allie said. "Maybe... maybe you're all too ugly?"

She pretended to cough to cover her laugh, unable to play that line deadpan, the way she wanted to... to see if they'd fall for it. Those boys, ugly? Not even when they were covered in dirt and hay and sweat. Hmmm... maybe it was the dirt, hay, and sweat that helped the cute cowboy factor along, instead of decreasing it.

"I told ya you guys were ugly!" Chris said. "Now you know."

The guys laughed, Bill too. Apparently one too many local girls had given those boys big heads. Ginger from the General Store probably had something to do with that, as well.

An upbeat song came on the playlist, and Allie grabbed Bill's hands. "We should dance."

"I don't dance," Bill said, but he kept his hands in hers.

"Well," she said, "I'm not going out there alone and putting on a show for you guys—"

"—it's not a *bad* idea," Eric joked good-naturedly. Zach pretended to slap Eric upside the head for it.

"—we need to make sure the dance floor's not too slippery for dancing!"

That sounded like a good reason, right? It had nothing to do with how much she enjoyed being with Bill, just being near him...working with him, smiling and laughing with him, pinning the food orders to the board in the kitchen as he worked his magic on the grill, and exchanging looks that only each other could understand—a skill that had come about from working so closely together on renovating the diner, and eating their meals together in his home for the past few weeks.

Bill stood, and let her drag him onto the dance floor. But once there, his whole demeanor changed. He took her hand, and immediately found his rhythm, leading her to dance with him.

Allie placed her hand on his broad shoulder, and whispered in his ear so that only he could hear. "You love working at the diner." It wasn't a question, it was just a fact.

"I do," he admitted. "I've been workin' a lot less on the ranch over the past couple years," he said. "Too many memories there. They keep me chained to the past."

She didn't have to ask to know exactly what (or rather, who) haunted Bill's memories over at Melody Ranch.

"And the work…" he added, "It doesn't get me goin' anymore."

He lowered his glance to her eyes, and Allie's breath caught in her throat, enjoying the feel of his complete attention.

"Don't get me wrong," Bill added, keeping his voice low so the guys couldn't overhear from the pool table in the back. "I love the land, I love the cattle, and the horses. But the day-to-day of ranchin' just… It's not somethin' I have my heart in, not anymore. Not for a while."

"If your heart's not in the ranch, then…where is it?" Allie whispered.

Say it's with me; please say your heart's with me.

She didn't know why she would want that, not when the idea frightened her. Somehow, she wanted it just the same.

"I think my heart's in makin' this diner a success now," Bill said. "I could see working here with you." He touched the rim of his hat. "That is…if you'd have me."

"Of course," she said. "Of course I'd have you, partner."

She smiled and whirled away from his embrace. They could be partners, and maybe, just maybe… something more.

Bill tugged her hand and she twirled back in against him, pressed against his chest.

"The dance floor," Bill said, "is jus' right."

They smiled at each other, faces beaming, and in that perfect moment all of her fears melted away. She was ready for this, for this new life with him.

What about Bill? Maybe he was ready for the diner, but was he ready for a relationship? Or would she forever only be… not his Melody?

Chapter Twelve

"IT'S GETTIN' REAL cold out there," Bill said.

He was upstairs from the diner in Allie's apartment with the guys, and while it still needed some cosmetic work, at least the bones of it were all well above code now.

Zach flushed the toilet one more time to make sure everything was hooked up properly, and came out of the bathroom to peer out the window in the living room.

"Those snow clouds, ya think?" Zach asked.

Bill scoffed without bothering to lift his head. "Too early."

Eric dropped the plaster he was using on the drywall, and peered out the window as well. "I don't know, boss, they look like rain clouds, but it's too cold for rain. If it comes down, it's gonna be a snow storm."

"What else do we have to do here, so that Allie can move in, and you can move *out*?" Zach asked.

Bill walked through the apartment, looking at everything carefully. The guys had done a really good job, and Allie had been helping with painting and picking up the furniture she would need from thrift stores and garage sales throughout the whole county.

"Looks real good," Bill said. "I think we just need to make sure she has a new refrigerator an' microwave."

The guys glanced at each other in uneasy silence.

"What?" Bill demanded.

Zach shrugged. "I bet you're ready for her to get out of your house, huh?" he asked. "She's been there a while now. Must be drivin' you crazy… since you like your space an' all."

Bill shrugged back in response. "I spend the nights here, anyway. Bein' with Allie the rest of the time, it ain't so bad."

"Bet you're looking forward to sleepin' in your own bed again," Chris said. "I mean…when Allie is sleeping in the apartment."

"Riiiight," Jay joked. Now the guys exchanged an altogether different look.

Bill could just imagine what they were thinking: *Bill an' Allie, sittin' in a tree, K-I-S-S-I-N-G.*

Bill laughed at the knowing expressions on their faces, and shook his head. "She's a good girl; she wouldn't let me even if I tried."

He wasn't going to spill his guts about Allie. It wasn't his style. The guys knew that he'd had his share of flings in the past two years. Those weren't girlfriends, though, and they weren't women he could fall for. They weren't even women that he had to see the next morning, if he didn't want to. It wasn't Christian of him to sleep with a woman he wasn't wed to, but after Melody died, none of that seemed to matter anymore. If God didn't care enough about him to at least protect his wife, than why would He care what Bill did in the time since?

But Allie was different. She was no virgin, clearly, as a divorcée, but despite the growing tenderness he felt for her, Bill knew better than to take advantage. It was one thing, allowing himself to fall into a downward spiral. He wasn't going to allow Allie to join him on the wrong path, as tempting as it was.

If God really did care as much as Allie thought He did, then…

No point in rehashing all that. The interruption of his thought process was a cold bucket of water, drowning the tiny spark of *If God, then…*

Well, one thing was for sure. Allie and Bill worked well together at the diner. He could actually see himself having a future there with her. The night they'd had their practice run with the guys at the diner had only proven what Bill already knew—his new venture with Allie was going to be a success. If only Uncle Freddy were around to see it, he would've loved it (once he got over grumbling about the girly aspects).

Grand opening was on Saturday night, only five days away.

Her apartment would be ready before then. Despite the fact that he'd never wanted her to take over his home, in the first place, Bill wished they could slow it all down. He wanted to keep Allie with him, at his house. Having her around had kind of…worked out.

Originally, he'd thought that he wouldn't want her in the same house with him, so that yeah, he could have his space. The guys knew all about that. Instead Bill felt like he could still have his own alone time, even when she was right there. Not because he shut her out, not at all. Maybe because she just seemed to belong there, with him. He didn't feel the need to escape her presence so that he could recharge, the way he did around everyone else.

At night, after the work was done, she would sit quietly, and read one of her books. Or she'd get up and bustle around, putting all his things in tidy piles so he couldn't find what he needed later. Funny how it didn't annoy him like he'd thought it would.

He usually took that as his cue to leave her be, and drive back to the apartment, where he fixed things up a little bit each night before crashing on the mattress.

Bill really cared about Allie, as a person. She'd been taking over his mind, to the point that... *he wasn't constantly thinking about Melody anymore.*

It almost felt like a new way of living... to not be consumed with thoughts of his late wife. Lately, it hadn't even been thoughts about Melody in particular, more like... guilt. Or anger.

It had been so long since Melody had been gone, that he had forgotten how her voice sounded, or what her hair felt like when he ran his fingers through the dark strands. That was something that had brought him a lot of shame, not remembering every detail of her time with him.

It didn't anymore. He would always feel sorrow that he'd lost his young bride so early, but it was a relief to have the grief lifted like clouds after a storm.

And behind the clouds, there was the sun. There was Allie Crawford.

Almost as if God had placed her in his life right when he needed her.

He'd never thought that he would have a future with a woman, but Allie had worked her way into his life so completely, that despite all of his plans to keep her at a distance, he found himself pulling her closer and closer toward him.

Now he didn't want her to move out of his house—not now that he had her there. Once she had her own place, she'd have no reason to visit him, to eat meals with him, or to sit on his couch and read while he got the fireplace going.

The only proper way to keep it going was to marry her. But neither of them wanted to do anything like that…right?

"Hey Bill," Zach said, interrupting his train of thought. "I bet we could have this apartment finished by tomorrow afternoon. I know for a fact that Chris's cousin has an old refrigerator in his yard that's doin' nobody any good. All we gotta do is screw the door back on."

Bill looked up in surprise. "The carpet needs to be replaced."

But what he really meant was… *I'm not ready to let her leave yet.*

Didn't matter, though—he couldn't keep Allie forever. He shouldn't want to, right? After all, he was the one who had insisted they be on the same page. And they were. She didn't want a relationship, and neither did he.

Man.

There was no way Bill was going to be the one to screw everything up by asking her to marry him so she would live with him, instead of in the apartment she had bought from him with her hard-earned money. It wouldn't be right, not once she had her own place to call home.

Zach looked at Bill, and raised his eyebrows. "Maybe you should talk to Allie about whether or not she's actually lookin' for new carpet right now, at all."

That cowboy was about as subtle as a hungry calf. Swap the word "carpet" with "relationship," (or maybe "ol' man") and that right there boiled down to the real question.

Bill smirked. "Ix-nay on the secret ode-cay."

"You've lost me," Zach said, smiling that lazy smile of his. "I was just talkin' 'bout carpet."

Allie's answer shouldn't matter to Bill. In fact, if Allie said anything other than "no, of course I'm not ready for a new man in my life," Bill might just run and hide under the bed like he'd done when he was four years old and scared of monsters.

How had this girl rewired his mind the way she did? He'd gone from thinking about Melody all the time, to comparing Allie to Melody, to now… thinking about Allie all the time instead. And with that, thinking about the things she held dear to her. Like her faith.

Was Allie his obsession now?

Bill had to be careful with his obsessions… it could consume him. If being with Allie was anything at all like his marriage to Melody, she would consume him completely, and then destroy him by tearing him down until he was nothing but dirt on the bottom of a boot.

"Let's get this apartment finished up fast for her, then," Bill said.

Even though it hurt him to say it.

* * *

The following afternoon, Bill stood in the doorway of the kitchen, holding his coffee mug and watching Allie run around like a crazy woman as she tried to find her keys.

She looked so cute, like a confused squirrel, darting back and forth, rechecking the same places twice. A lock of her blonde hair came loose from her braid, and fell across her cheek.

Allie caught his gaze and flashed him an annoyed look. "Are you enjoying your coffee?"

"The coffee, and the free entertainment." Bill laughed, and set the mug down so he could help her search.

"Nice," she said, but he could see her trying to hide her smile.

"You shouldn't be goin' out in the snow," Bill said, "anyways."

The guys were already setting up the wood-burning stoves in the barns, and putting up some make-shift covered areas for the cattle who needed it. The temperatures were dropping into the single digits at night now.

"I still haven't seen the new carpet!" Allie said. "Besides, I have to learn how to drive in the snow at some point. Hardy Idaho women aren't afraid of a little weather."

"That what you are now?" Bill asked with a smirk. "Where'd the Miami girl go?"

He crossed the room into her bedroom and grabbed her keys from the top of her dresser, which was the fourth most common place she liked to leave them.

"Thank you!" She grabbed the keys from his hand, their touch accidental, but still electric, enticing.

Just a touch wasn't enough. An overwhelming sense of protectiveness and... something else... came over him.

Bill wrapped his arm around her waist and pulled her toward him.

She looked up at him with a small smile and laughed a little. "Yes?"

"It's good everythin's fixed at your apartment," Bill said. "But our Grand Opening is comin' up real soon—no reason to add the hassle of movin' on top of that."

He took a breath, unsatisfied with the expression on Allie's face, which hadn't changed since she'd grabbed the keys from his hand.

Allie raised her eyebrows. "I have to move out. Give you back your space."

"*Stay with me.*" His voice was thick with unexpected emotion, and she smiled weakly as she shook her head, as if to soften the blow.

"I can't… I can't just live here while you spend the nights at the apartment." Her smile faltered. "I mean, I can't continue to. Not when there's any other choice, it just wouldn't be right. People are probably already talking about how we spend all day together. Besides, I'm sure I drive you crazy."

"Oh, you drive me crazy all right…"

"I'm driving myself crazy too," Allie said with a short laugh. "I don't even know what I'm doing here…"

If only he could read her mind. Did she mean here, in his arms? Maybe here in Idaho. Or in his house.

Allie shook her head and smiled, as if to clear her thoughts. "It's barely snowing out," she said. "I'm going to head over to the diner, check out what you guys have done with the apartment and make a list of anything else I need there, and try calling around again for someone to perform on Saturday night."

"I told ya you'd have a hard time gettin' a musician. Bear Creek Saddle's not exactly filled with rock stars."

Allie waved her hand, as if to shoo away his words. "All the ads we have on flyers and message boards around town say we're having live music. So we're having live music, even if I have to fly someone up from Hollywood to make it happen!"

Bill laughed, hoping at least that that was a joke. He had no intention of paying someone to fly all the way up from Los Angeles to sing at their small diner… in an even smaller town… in the middle of nowhere. Hard to think that was a possibility.

"You're comin' back for dinner here, right?" he asked.

"Of course," she said. "Well…I guess I don't have to put you out anymore. Not if everything is fixed up there...I could bring an overnight bag and—"

"Kitchen's not even stocked there," Bill interrupted. "Come back here for dinner. I'll cook."

"You're really not sick of me yet?" she teased.

"House won't be the same without you in it," Bill said. He just needed her to know that... that he needed her.

She jingled the keys, grabbed her purse and was out the door with a smile.

There were no visible stars out. It had been getting dark so early in the day, and tonight not even the moon had found a hole in the clouds to shine through. The snow wasn't bad now, but if living in north Idaho his whole life had taught Bill anything, it was how to tell when the weather was going to get worse.

"I shouldn't've let her go," he mumbled to himself.

Not like he had any choice. Allie was her own woman, as she liked to let him know all the time, both in action and words.

He needed her... and that couldn't happen, not ever again. It was as if he'd been underwater for the past two years, maybe even longer... maybe since Melody had stopped talking with him, and started distancing herself, day by day. Bit by bit.

He had lost himself; he'd been drowning. Treading water, losing air. And once Melody had gotten in that crash, Bill had just...gone under.

He'd been a dead man walking for these past two years, but God had thrown him a life vest with that very first email Allie sent.

Now he was above water again—man, he was swimming toward the boat and ready to step onto dry land. But now that he was out of the water, he was afraid to ever go back in again.

He shouldn't need Allie, couldn't need her —

Because if he did, she would lure him back into the water like a mythical Siren, and this time... he would drown.

Chapter Thirteen

A LLIE WIPED HER boots off on the welcome mat outside Uncle Freddy's Diner, and took the separate entrance that went directly in to the stairwell that led up to her apartment. There was no fear ascending the stairs now, not like the first time she'd gone. The small one-bedroom suite was quite cheery and homey now, despite its previous state, and despite being above the diner.

One of the best things about it that she hadn't taken the time to appreciate before, was that the floor and walls were soundproofed, so even if she was upstairs while people were in the diner getting rowdy, she wouldn't hear it. It wasn't something that worried her now, but maybe in the future, when things really got going, she'd be able to hire some help and have some off days or nights.

And wow, the new carpet looked awesome. It was one of those carpets that matched everything, super plush under her bare feet, and had even been treated to repel stains. Pretty much the perfect carpet.

Allie walked through and made notes in her phone about the things she still had to pick up: dishtowels, laundry detergent for the tiny stacked washer and dryer, matching lampshades for the bedroom (since the actual lamp stands didn't match), and maybe some scented candles… That might help reduce the new carpet and paint smell.

She flung herself back onto her queen-sized bed, and stared out the window. The heavy curtains were still open from when Zach and the guys had last been in there, working. The security light outside her building illuminated the falling snow.

Bill asked me to stay with him.

"Did you mean it?" Allie whispered, scarcely aware she'd spoken out loud in the empty room.

She believed that he meant it when he'd said, "stay until after the opening." But did he actually want to live with her on a more…permanent basis? What kind of relationship would that mean for them?

Were they to be platonic housemates?

Because with the way she felt toward him, the only way they could live together would be if he put a ring on her finger. Not like that was going to happen.

Staying chaste was getting harder due to their proximity. There was a reason she hadn't lived with her ex-husband before they got married. It would have been too difficult.

Theoretically, if she and Bill planned on living together for real, as man and wife, she could always rent out the apartment above the diner for extra money. It wouldn't be a financial loss in that sense, even if she had spent her savings on buying the place. Or maybe, since Bill had said he had too many bad memories there at Melody Ranch, he could even move in with her at the diner.

Whoa. This was moving too fast.

But as fast as it was moving, it also seemed… right. Would Bill consider living with her, here? She looked around the bedroom. It wasn't too girly, not like Melody's room in Bill's house. It was the type of room a man could feel comfortable in. She touched the pillow on the side of the bed next to her. What would it be like, to have Bill lying there with her, every night?

What would it be like, to have Bill Edwards at her disposal—to be able to be with him, take care of him and have him take care of her—as they both worked together at the diner?

Outside the window, it was all snow, no stars. "I don't need a star to wish on," she whispered out loud. "Lord, if you have a plan for me, let me do it right. Your way. I want to be with Bill. But I have no idea if that's what You want."

She sighed. If Bill wanted to live with her, he'd have to marry her. And based on everything he'd said, that wasn't in her future.

It was comforting having Bill around in the house at the ranch when she was home. Not having him here in this little apartment with her made it seem too empty, as if it wasn't really her home, after all.

That's got to just be because it was new to her. It wouldn't take more than a few weeks for the apartment to feel like home, right? With or without Bill. She could already envision herself cozying up on the couch (bought used at the church thrift shop, but new to her and in great shape), with a fuzzy blanket and a cup of tea and a good book. She even had an end-table in the perfect spot to set the mug down and put a reading lamp on it.

She added "reading lamp for end-table" to the notes in her phone.

The snow was coming down quicker, and Allie checked the time. What had seemed like only twenty-five minutes in the apartment had actually been over an hour and a half. She grabbed her purse and keys, and bundled up before heading outside.

A blanket of snow covered everything, making it all beautiful and clean. There wasn't a scraper in her car (did they even sell ice-scrapers in Florida?) so she put the car's defrost on with the heat turned up to full blast, and sat in the cold driver's seat, waiting for it to melt.

She loved that new apartment, and she loved the diner. She couldn't wait for opening day, and to share that day with Bill. What she wanted most of all was to go home to Bill right now, take off her coat, and warm up her feet. Sitting with their books by the fireplace sounded completely ideal right about now. They'd eat dinner, and after a while, he'd head out to spend the night at the apartment.

He didn't seem worried about driving in the snow later, and the roads were bound to be worse by then, so why should she be concerned?

She was a proper Idaho citizen now, after all. Snow didn't stop Idahoans for a second.

When she could see well enough out the mostly-defrosted windshield, Allie opened the car door and stepped back outside into the bitter cold. Her gloved hands weren't as good as a scraper, but she wanted to push as much of the snow off the car as she could.

The ice beneath her feet surprised her, and her foot came out under her. She would've slipped if she hadn't been holding onto the car door.

"Goodness!" she gasped. That had been a close one. It was definitely icy out. The snow seemed to freeze the moment it hit the already-icy pavement.

Bill had said something about how the town would salt and

sand the streets for better traction, but there were no plows out on the road now.

Allie got in the car and shivered until the blasting air from the heat warmed her. She put her car into gear, and—very slowly—started the relatively short drive back to Melody Ranch.

"Steady, steady," she murmured. The car didn't listen.

Her tires spun on the slick road. Thank God there were no other cars out, or she would've hit somebody for sure, swerving into both sides of the road as she did despite her best efforts to keep the car in line.

Each time the tires skidded, Allie's stomach dropped. *Bill was right*. She shouldn't have gone out in the snow—especially since she knew nothing about how to drive in snow.

Hardy Idaho woman, hah. You could take the girl out of Miami, but you couldn't take the Miami-driver out of the girl, apparently.

Her car wasn't equipped for this, either. Why hadn't she asked for a loan to get those studded tires everyone else was talking about at the ranch? Bill would've done it. She'd been too prideful to even think of asking.

Now she was in trouble.

She had to turn left, so she slowed down even more and put the car into a lower gear.

"Just turn the way I want you to," she warned the car.

Though she drove at a turtle's pace, the car was all over the road, even after making the turn (sort of).

"Come on!"

This was a rear-wheel drive vehicle. And there had definitely been some mention that rear-wheel drive was not good in the snow—

The car skidded, spinning on the black ice.

No no no no no

Allie shrieked, unable to stop the sound from leaving her mouth.

Take a deep breath. Focus.

She willed the car to stop, trying to control the spinning steering wheel even though she had no idea what on earth she was doing. Was she supposed to steer into the spin? Away from it? Which way was that?

"Come on, come on," she muttered. Adrenaline coursed through her body.

The pine tree on her right was dangerously close. The thick trunk with its heavy green pine needles sagging under a layer of snow filled her field of vision; it was all she could see. The car seemed drawn toward the tree by a gravitational pull. It was as if her car and that tree made a mutual decision to just—

CRASH!

Dear God—

Allie yanked the wheel to the left at the last split-second to keep the impact from being a head-on collision. Her airbag inflated, and knocked her head back against the head rest. It all happened at the same time, and it was over in an instant.

Help! Where was her cowboy to pick her up out of danger and toss her over his saddle?

"Bill," she cried out, although in her mind, she'd thought she'd yelled for help. Maybe she'd done both.

Allie's head hurt, just a bit. It didn't feel life-threatening. Allie swallowed her fear and batted the deflating airbag out of her way. With a shaky breath, she looked around.

The car, the wheel, the tires—everything that had been spinning so fast was now still. *One step at a time.* She put it in park, and put the parking brake on.

Time to assess the damage. She was *okay*. Alive, no matter how scary the collision had been.

Thank you, Jesus...

Her head hurt where the airbag had hit her, and her chest hurt where the shoulder strap of the seatbelt had pressed into her, keeping her from being ejected through the glass. Her left thumb, of all random things, hurt the worst.

Allie pulled her head back against the headrest and closed her eyes. The street was silent all around her, as if the horrifying crunch of steel compacting against bark, of glass shattering, hadn't been the only thing that filled her ears only moments ago.

"Thank you, Lord," she said, her eyes closed, her breath finally returning to normal. "That could have been really bad. Really bad. But I'm okay—thank you, thank you."

* * *

Bill didn't like waiting around. It was snowing too hard out now for Allie to make it home in her rear-wheel drive car, especially since she had zero experience driving in bad weather. He had tried to call her cell phone to let her know he was coming to pick her up—that he could drive her home, they could get her car in the morning, after the roads had been plowed and salted—but she didn't answer.

Maybe her phone had died. Maybe she was getting ready to leave right now, completely oblivious to the driving conditions.

Forget waiting around for a call. Bill was going to pick her up, whether Allie wanted him to or not. She'd be safer driving home as a passenger in his four-wheel-drive truck than she would be trying to navigate the icy roads herself.

He had to slip metal treads over his boots to make it into his truck without falling.

His truck already had studded tires on and was doing fine. Why hadn't he insisted she change her tires? Why hadn't he just done it for her without her asking?

Bill was halfway to the diner when he saw—

No. No Dear Lord No No

—the passenger-side of Allie's little blue car with Florida plates was crashed up against a thick evergreen tree. Broken pine branches and glass littered the road and the sidewalk.

God don't do this to me—

Bill jumped out of his truck before it had even rolled to a stop, hoping the metal treads on his heavy boots would keep him from sliding on the slick road. He could see her... her head was back, her eyes closed. In the driver side.

A car crash.

It could NOT happen again NO it could NOT happen AGAIN—

"Allie, please—" he said, throwing the door of her car open.

Allie's eyes opened and her head snapped up in surprise. She winced at the sudden movement, then smiled.

"Bill—you're here!"

He didn't know whether to laugh or to cry—*she's alive!*—and it came out as a strangled laugh somehow, his eyes burning with unshed tears at the horror he'd thought he might have walked up on.

"You crashed," he gasped, barely able to get the words out. His throat was too tight.

"Oh Bill—I'm so sorry," she said.

She looked more concerned about him than made sense. She was the one who had just wrecked, yet she was apologizing.

"No, *I'm* sorry," he said. "God, I'm so sorry." He swallowed hard, trying to loosen the constriction in his throat. "Are you okay?" he asked, urgency in his voice.

"I'm fine," she said, and she sounded like she meant it. "The car's not, though."

Bill put his hands inside the car, carefully feeling her neck, her spine, running down her whole body, checking for injuries the way he had learned to do back when he was a volunteer firefighter.

"Does it hurt here?" he asked as he checked her out.

"No," Allie said. "I really am fine. I think I hurt my thumb... don't know how."

She unbuckled her lap belt, and carefully stepped out of the car. The thumb on her left hand was already beginning to swell.

Bill wrapped his arms around her, and hugged her, resisting the urge to squeeze her as tightly as he could, because he didn't want to hurt her.

"I'm so glad you're all right," he said fiercely. "You gave me a scare."

"Did you see the crash?"

"I saw you... with your eyes closed —" his voice broke.

"I'm so sorry I scared you," she said. "You can see yourself, I'm totally fine."

He nodded, swallowing hard, tightening his hug around her despite himself. "A part of me died inside the moment I saw you like that."

"I was just praying, Bill," she whispered. "I had my eyes closed because I was literally thanking God that I was fine," she said. "So bring that little part inside of you back to life, okay?"

She smiled up at him reassuringly, as if to remind him that she was *all right*. She was not his Melody.

Bill held her injured hand in his, inspecting it. "I bet that airbag broke your thumb at the same time it saved your life."

"Don't be dramatic," Allie said softly. "The tree hit the side of the car, I was wearing my seatbelt, and I had airbags. It's just one of those things. I'm fine. I'm here."

He walked her carefully back to his truck, and lifted her up so she didn't have to pull herself up onto the high-up seat.

"I hope you have some aspirin or something at the ranch," Allie said, cradling her hand.

Bill stared straight ahead as he drove, concentrating on getting to the hospital two towns over, safely. "Gettin' you checked out tonight," he said. He would accept no argument on that. "And I'll call Joe to tow your car tomorrow."

Allie's hand shook as she wrapped her arms around herself in the passenger seat. It must be from the adrenaline rush she'd experienced during the crash.

"No point in fixin' up that car," Bill told her. "What's good in Miami isn't any good in north Idaho. You need somethin' with four-wheel drive and studded tires."

That was the last thing he said to her for the rest of the night. It wasn't on purpose... he just...

Car crash. It was as if his past was coming back to remind him that he'd messed up. Messed up by daring to think he had a future ahead of him with Allie.

She could be taken from him at any moment. That was

something he knew now, knew for sure. And surely Allie too must know—since her husband left her—that Bill could leave her at any moment, as well.

It was impossible to bare one's heart to another when you know too much.

And Bill… he knew too much.

* * *

Allie wrapped a plastic bag around her casted hand, and let it drape over the side of the tub as she soaked away the tension from her body.

The car crash had frightened her, yes—but what had frightened her more was Bill's reaction to it. She'd triggered him, and he'd gone into survival mode it seemed. It was like he was on autopilot. Once he knew she was okay, it was as if he'd shut off.

Completely detached from her, both emotionally and physically.

Yes, he'd taken care of her. Taken her to the hospital, stayed with her the whole time until he was able to drive her home, and make her a grilled cheese sandwich.

He had turned the radio on to the news, to cover the growing silence in the house. Not the comfortable silence they enjoyed as they sat together eating breakfast and sharing parts of the Bear Creek Saddle Gazette, or sitting and reading, sharing the same throw-blanket, her feet on his lap.

No… the silence had been different. It said… *I have something to say that I can't…so I won't.* Or maybe just, *There are too many thoughts swirling in my head to know what to say… so I will say nothing.*

She hoped she was wrong. Maybe Bill was just scared, and tired.

Obviously seeing a car crash was going to trigger him to think about losing his wife. But that didn't mean he was done with Allie, right? It had only been a few hours before, that they were smiling with each other in the hallway, and he had invited her to stay at his house for a while longer.

Stay with me.

That's what he had told her. And it scared her too, it went against every protective instinct she had, to put herself in a position to be emotionally injured by a man again. Still… if it turned out that Bill was scared of being with her now because of the crash— because of all the bad memories it brought bubbling to the surface—then she would have to tell him the same thing.

Stay with me.

Chapter Fourteen

ALLIE AWOKE EARLY the morning after the car crash, aching all over. She popped one of the few extra-strength non-narcotic pain pills the doctor at the emergency room had prescribed to her to use for the first week or so, until the pain in her broken thumb and the muscle aches subsided.

It took a little longer than usual to get dressed with only one good hand. How was she going to waitress at the Grand Opening party?

Allie limped to the kitchen for coffee, despite not having injured her lower body at all. Just annoying muscle cramps left over from tensing every bit of her body during the impact. It was as if her body was saying "What did you do to me??"

Ugh. She might be off her game, but at least she could be off her game and *caffeinated*.

One of Bill's socks was on the floor, probably dropped either on its way into or out of the laundry room. Wincing, she leaned down and picked it up. A pair of his shorts was also on the floor.

She picked up another couple of small items of clothing as she followed the trail into the back of the small house, to his bedroom.

The door to his room lay open, which was unusual for Bill. Maybe with his arms full of laundry, he just hadn't been able to shut it.

"You dropped some," Allie said, standing in the doorway.

"Just put it on the bed with the rest."

Something was wrong between them, still. Bill was behaving differently around her, distancing himself ever since the accident last night. Practically ignoring her.

"It's not your usual laundry day," she noted. "Something up?"

"No. Nothin'."

Bill folded the clean clothes from the dryer with slow, methodical skill. It wasn't strange that her jack-of-all-trades cowboy could keep house, too, but she'd never have guessed it by looking at him.

Allie walked over to the bed where he had all his clothes piled up, and picked up one of his big black T-shirts. She folded it and set it to the side, reaching for another shirt.

"If you really want to help," Bill said, "you can put the folded ones in there."

He pointed to a big duffel bag—green-drab and probably from the Army surplus store in town—on the floor by his bed.

"What's going on?" she asked.

Fear and anxiety twisted her stomach. There was no reason for Bill to be packing. Where did he think he was going? They had a future together. A diner to open in only three days.

"Your apartment is ready for you to move into," Bill said quietly. "You need to get your stuff together as well. I'll help you move everything over tonight."

"Tonight?" Adrenaline rushed through her, making all of her pain disappear. "That's it? You're just… kicking me out?"

"I'm not kicking you out," Bill said. "You bought that

apartment when you bought your half of the diner. It's where you're s'posed to live."

The clothes… the duffel bag. "Are you… moving as well?" she asked in confusion.

This couldn't be the end. Why did he want her to leave? It didn't matter that the apartment was hers. She liked living with him, being with him.

Why couldn't he just ask her to marry him? Would she even want that?

Yes. Desperately.

Bill shook his head. "I can't do this, Allie. I thought I could, but that was stupid of me." He took a breath, his strong hands gripping the laundry, wrinkling it. "For a little while there, I thought… man. My past don't matter if I can be with—have the diner with—you."

Allie grabbed his hands, making him drop the balled-up shirt onto the floor. "That's true, Bill. That's *still* true. So why are you kicking me out?"

"I was wrong about everythin'," Bill said. "*I can't do this.* You have to move out—into your own apartment. I'm goin' to sell the ranch to Zach and the guys…it should be theirs anyways. And you… I'm gonna let you buy out my half of the diner. You can own it yourself."

Her head reeled from all of the information he had just thrown at her at once. "I can't afford to buy the whole diner," she said. "But that doesn't matter right now… I understand wanting to sell the ranch, since now we have the diner, together. But if you sell me the diner *and* you sell your ranch, what do you have left? What are you going to do?"

Bill shrugged, gently extracting himself from her hold on his hands.

A sudden fear gripped her. He was getting rid of everything. "You're not going to do anything crazy, are you?"

"I've got a huntin' cabin I haven't used in too long. It's deeper into the mountain. Less people. With a little work, I can live there full-time." He paused, avoiding her stare. "I'm better off on my own."

His words hit her like a slap in the face. Allie could run now, and hold onto her dignity. But she couldn't let him go without a fight. He had to know she *wanted* him. Needed him.

"This is all because of me," she said, her voice breaking. "We have something good, Bill. You don't have to ruin it all." Tears welled up in her eyes but she fought them back. "Please don't leave."

"You could've died, Allie!" Bill grabbed her shoulders, his grey eyes finally looking directly into her own. "Don't you see that?"

She flinched, frightened by the intensity in his gaze, at how firmly he held her in his iron grasp. But he didn't shake her, didn't hurt her. At least not with his hands.

"If you hadn't been wearin' your seatbelt," he said, his voice raising, "if you hadn't turned the wheel at the last second, or if any other *dozens of factors* hadn't worked perfectly the way they did—you would be *dead* right now. I can't lose you like that, Allie." His face was flushed, his voice raw with emotion.

"It's okay," she whispered, trying to comfort him. "I'm not even really afraid of dying. There are worse things than getting called Home. It just wasn't my time."

"Yes, there are worse things," he growled. "Like being the one left behind. And that scares the daylights out of me."

"But I didn't die," Allie said, "I wasn't even close. I'm fine. I walked away with a little tiny fractured thumb." She tried to smile, to prove just how okay she was, but she couldn't.

"I tried, Allie," Bill said, dropping his hands from her shoulders. "I tried to see, what would it be like to let myself get close to you. But it's not worth it, it ain't worth the pain. At any moment I could lose you. You could lose me... just like you lost your own husband, fool that he was when he left you."

Tears stung Allie's eyes. "Yes. I'm fully aware when you're in a relationship with somebody you care about, there's always a chance you could lose them at any time."

It was something that had stopped Allie before. But it wouldn't now. "I'm not willing to live in fear, not anymore," she said. "Our diner's grand opening is on Saturday! I want you with me, by my side. Please, Bill."

Bill shook his head slowly. "It's just like with Melody, all over again. I can't do it. I won't do it. You can have the diner...forget the money. I'll sign it over to you."

At any other time in her life, Allie would have been ecstatic to hear those words—that she could be the sole owner of her business. But not now, not like this.

"I don't want your half of the diner," she said, her voice breaking. "I want you. I want you there, as my partner."

But Bill didn't seem to be listening. He was back to the task on hand like an automaton, folding clothes, putting them in his bag. One after another.

"When are you leaving?" she whispered.

"'Bout a week or so. I still need to work out the details of deeding Melody Ranch over to Zach Walker and the guys 'fore I leave for good." He paused, as if realizing he might be giving her false hope by saying he wasn't moving for another week. "But Allie—I *am* gonna help you move to your apartment tonight."

She opened her mouth to protest, but he gave her a look that stopped her cold.

"You can't say no to this," Bill said. "You have no right."

"I don't care," she whispered, her throat strained from keeping all her emotions from bursting out of her. "I'm still saying no."

"If you think you can just keep on sleepin' here, you can bet I'm takin' my own bed back. I'll be sleeping here too and then we'd be practically livin' in sin," he said. "That's what half the town'll think. You don't want that."

"We're not behaving like we're married," she countered, "we're just friends—"

"You don't feel like just a friend," he admitted. "Just because we ain't sharing a bed don't mean there's nothing between us and you know it."

Her denial stuck in her throat. Yes, she knew it. He was right. As much as it hurt, he was right.

She had prayed for God to show her His will, and now He was showing her. It just wasn't the answer she'd wanted.

"Until I sell Melody Ranch, this is still my house," Bill said, his voice cold. Firm. "And I'm revokin' my invitation for you to be a guest in it. You have your own apartment. Get your things together."

She wanted to scream. To cry. To break things. To pound on his chest and yell at him for being so very cruel. Her beautiful cowboy really was Big Bad Bill, after all.

She lifted her chin, even though it quivered. She strode out of his bedroom, waiting until she was in the privacy of her room—Melody's room—to cry.

It's over, over before it began. He didn't want her…and she couldn't say no to that, either.

This is my fault. If she hadn't gone out in the snow, against the advice of a man who clearly knew more about snow than a girl from Miami who just wanted to look at some stupid new carpet —

Arrgh… If only she hadn't gotten into that car crash… If she hadn't, this wouldn't have happened.

No. Allie ran her hands over her face, swiping at the tears. His rejection would've happened sooner or later. It was probably best for Bill to stop their relationship now, before they both got in too deep.

He was protecting himself, and in doing so, he was trying to protect her, too.

Only one problem… Allie was *already* in too deep. Bill couldn't protect her from a broken heart… because he'd just broken it.

Chapter Fifteen

ALLIE DIDN'T HAVE much to unpack in her new apartment. Since Bill had dropped her off three nights ago, she'd had plenty of time to put away her clothing, and put up a few pictures she'd brought with her.

The three boxes of belongings she brought with her from Miami helped make the apartment feel more like home. It was definitely nice to be in a place she had decorated herself, instead of a room decorated by Bill's late wife.

Maybe Bill had a point. That house was filled with memories… It was impossible to escape Melody, at Melody Ranch.

Tonight was the Grand Opening party for Uncle Freddy's Diner. Allie had her outfit picked out, she had the diner ready, including a playlist for background music and a menu of specials written in chalk above the counter.

Everything was set, except for the live music. She'd been making phone calls all last week, and even though it was Saturday and now completely last minute, she was still calling around. The local high school in the next town over (some of the locals were bussed over there, since Bear Creek Saddle was too small for its own school district) apparently had a pretty good garage band, but they couldn't come because their lead singer was playing football at an away-game. So that was out. It was beginning to look hopeless.

No. It's already hopeless.

There would be no live music, and while Bill agreed to work the kitchen, he was already training a couple of local guys to replace him. If they were already up to par, he probably would not be attending the opening of his own diner. Also, her hand was casted past her wrist because her stupid thumb was broken, which meant carrying heavy trays was probably out, too. Awesome.

I miss him. None of it worked without him.

Did any of it even matter if she didn't have Bill by her side?

From the moment they had first begun emailing with each other, Allie had felt that undeniable connection with this man across the country, and she knew… he'd felt it too. With the relative anonymity of the internet, they had been able to get to know each other faster, and deeper, than if they'd just met by chance in real life—like at a diner.

How ironic that it was a diner that actually brought them together in the first place.

Yeah, he'd been a major jerk when she'd first arrived. And he was acting like one now, too—albeit for different, more noble reasons. It'd been so silly of her to think she'd never fall for that handsome cowboy just because he was such a jerk. Big Bad Bill had stolen her heart, and now she was at a loss for what to do about it.

I love him.

The realization struck her hard, and she sat straighter in her chair, setting the phone down.

How had she even entertained the idea of marrying him just to live with him, to be with him, without examining her heart?

How, after promising herself—no, *vowing*—that she would

never fall in love again, how had she let her guard down to the point that she'd let Bill sneak in under the radar?

He was *broken*, he had said so himself. Just because he was handsome, and a good man deep down, and adopted wounded horses… just because he could make her laugh, and made her feel things she'd never felt before… Just because Bill understood her on a deep, personal level—that did *not* mean that she loved him and should be together with him as a couple. That didn't mean anything at all, right?

No. It meant *everything*.

I'm in love with Bill Edwards.

Despite her best intentions not to, despite her very real knowledge of how much it hurt to lose someone you love, Allie had messed up. She'd messed up by falling in love with the one man who would never, ever, love her back.

Bill seemed so sure Allie was dangerous the way Melody was. That Allie had the power to destroy him, to break him completely just like he'd told her would happen. She didn't want that power— to take a strong man and crush the remaining ability to love that he'd held on to.

He could keep that for himself…she would trust him with it. Allie didn't need it, didn't want it.

She just wanted Bill. All of him, and all of his heart.

Lord, please soften his heart toward me. If that's what You want. You know it's what I want. "I pray in Jesus' name," she whispered.

Her throat hurt from swallowing back every word she'd been wanting to say, but now it came pouring out. She kept praying, holding fast to the knowledge that no matter what, she had His love to count on.

* * *

Bill stroked Pirate's face, between his eyes. The black stallion had come to trust him, and Bill felt comfortable with the horse in turn.

"I didn't think I'd be able to tame you," he admitted to Pirate. "You surprised me."

Bill opened the gate, and led Pirate out. Saddling Pirate was no longer a death-defying task. The horse's wound had healed cleanly, and during that time, Bill and Pirate had gotten to know each other. Pirate wasn't so quick to freak out anymore. It was like he knew, instinctually, that Bill wasn't going to hurt him.

If only Bill could feel the same way toward Allie. Allie *could* hurt him. If he let her, she would. It was no wonder he was still wild at heart, escaping to even deeper into the mountains, to live alone.

"You can come with me," Bill said to the stallion. "We can keep each other company."

He would be glad to leave Melody Ranch in the very capable hands of Zach Walker, and Eric Hunt, Chris Green, and Jay Thomas. Solid ranchers, all of them. Hopefully, the guys would not take after Bill's footsteps and live their lives alone forever. They were good guys; they deserved happiness—wives, and children. A *life*. Everything that Bill had thought he would have with Melody, until it was taken from him.

The way he felt about Allie though… it was different. Stronger, somehow, than he'd ever felt even about his own wife. How messed up was that? He was supposed to have loved Melody, his wife, forever.

Until death do us part.

Yeah. Only until "death do us part"—but that was easier said than done. For the longest time, every brief date he had after Melody was gone—seeking comfort if only for a short while by spending time with a pretty woman—had felt like a betrayal. Maybe it was.

But… he wasn't hurting anyone, morally, by falling for Allie. Surely Melody, unhappy and depressed as she was during her last few months on earth as his wife, wouldn't expect him to remain on his own forever. Melody hadn't planned on being Bill's wife, and she hadn't wanted to live on her namesake ranch.

Too many memories, most of them hard to deal with. Really hard. He wished he could seal off his past and forget all about it.

But Allie kept bringing it back up. Just having her there, knowing that he… he loved her.

I love Allie.

"I'm in serious trouble," he muttered to Pirate, who looked at him quizzically. Bill finished strapping the saddle on, and hopped up on to the stallion.

"Hup!" he ordered, and squeezed his thighs against the horse's muscular body.

Pirate responded in return, and Bill urged him toward the trail in the area near the woods. They moved together smoothly, the muscles in Bill's thighs and calves flexing right along with the horse's huge body, and soon they were trotting quickly, not quite galloping—not yet.

What had he done? *I love Allie.*

She had almost died. He would've had to have gone through everything all over again. Everything that he'd experienced with Melody, only times a million, because Bill felt even more deeply about Allie than he'd ever thought humanly possible. He loved Allie in a way he hadn't known existed.

He had thought he had already felt true love in the highest form—yet Allie still superseded everything.

And Allie even wanted to be with him. She wanted to spend time with Bill. She wanted Bill with her, at the grand opening. If Bill could have hand-picked a woman to be the exact opposite of his late wife, in the hopes of avoiding a similar unhappily one-sided relationship, he would have picked Allie.

So why was the fear still there?

Bill looked out at the setting sun. The snow from last week had mostly melted, though still thick up higher in the mountains, where his hunting cabin waited for him. The Grand Opening of Uncle Freddy's Diner was the talk of the town. Everyone would be there. Every teenager in town was booked to babysit the younger kids, so the parents could go to the big party. It had been over a year in the making—folks were excited.

And Bill would not be working there after tonight. He *should* be there. It was Allie's diner, through and through—no matter what the deed said. He didn't feel like he should own half of that. He really did want to sell it to Allie, so she could claim the whole thing as her own.

He didn't care anymore if the diner was out of his family. It wasn't as if Bill had children, or even nieces or nephews, to pass the diner down to the way Uncle Freddy had done with him.

He had no legacy to leave anyone.

But that could change.

I love Allie Crawford.

And she actually… maybe she even loved him too. He couldn't

be sure. He couldn't even imagine why somebody as amazing as Allie, someone as smart and beautiful and *good* as Allie would want him. He'd been so horrible to her. The way he'd spoken to her when she'd arrived, it made him sick to think back on it. Man, it had only been a few days ago that he'd kicked her out of his house and yelled at her.

There was no way Allie could love him back. It wouldn't make any sense.

Indecision tore him in two. He squeezed his thighs tighter and yelled at Pirate to go hard. Pirate didn't need to be told twice. Bill pushed forward into a gallop, leaned forward and galloped fast, faster, letting the cold night air run over him.

There were two paths he could take—not the dirt paths in front of him, the ones he could ride with his eyes closed. It was the direction his entire life could go that tormented him.

He could go up into the mountain, go to his cabin and live out his life alone. His heart would be safe. But it would only be safe because he wouldn't be using it. And what was the point of protecting himself from hurt, if he wasn't living anyway? What kind of a life would he have if Allie wasn't in it?

Please, God, show me what to do...

His choice became clear. The scary, unknown path was the only right choice. Whether Allie felt the same way as he did, or whether she wanted him out of her life for good...Bill had to tell her that he loved her.

That future he had envisioned with her, working at the diner with her, living with each other... sleeping together in each other's arms, every night.

He couldn't let all of his fears get in the way of that. Yes, she had gotten into a car accident. And that sure had triggered a lot of bad memories. And brought up a lot of fears.

Allie is not Melody.

She was her own woman. Bill knew now that he loved her, and he wanted to be with her despite everything that had gone wrong in his past, and that might go wrong in the future. He wanted her.

And God willing, that woman would want him back.

Chapter Sixteen

ALLIE LOOKED AROUND the diner with excitement. The party was everything she'd dreamed of. The grand opening had drawn everyone in town, it seemed. Well, obviously not everyone —there was no way that 648 people could fit in the space—but the place was packed. The cool thing was, men had brought their wives, men brought their dates, and even Zach and the other ranch hands had some girls from town on their arms.

A young woman with blonde hair and a former-cheerleader smile came up to Allie at the diner.

"I'm Paige," she said, needing to raise her voice to go over the music and the din of the crowd. "Zach was telling me about how you and Bill were fixing up this place. I love it!"

"Thank you!" Allie said, shaking the girl's hand. "I'm definitely going for a more female-friendly vibe here."

"It's working! I'd totally come here with my girlfriends."

Paige flashed her a big smile and was sucked back into the crowd, where she attached herself to Zach's hip. Zach didn't seem particularly into her, though. And he had told Allie that he was still looking for a girlfriend… for a wife.

Where was that cowboy going to find someone new to date, if he was taking over Melody Ranch and staying put in Bear Creek

Saddle? Poor Zach.

"Isn't this great?" Ginger yelled over the diner, raising her voice to be heard over the people chattering.

"I couldn't have done it without you," Allie said.

Since Ginger's General Store was the place everyone went to shop other than the big Walmart two towns over, having Ginger tell each and every customer about the renovation and grand opening certainly had to have made a big difference.

"On the house," Allie said, handing her a cold fountain soda, "as a thank you."

Ginger beamed. "Thanks! So…what have you been doing to Big Bad Bill? He hasn't been nearly as horrible around town lately." She paused, sipping the soda. "Come to think of it, just the fact that he's around town lately at all is out of character for him."

"Where's Bill at, anyway?" a guy asked from down the counter.

He was only the twentieth person to ask her that in the past hour that the party had been going strong.

"Bill got everything started in the kitchen earlier, and now the other guys are handling the orders," Allie explained. "But I think he's coming back soon."

That had been her standard answer. She didn't have the heart to tell them that Bill didn't want anything to do with the Uncle Freddy's Diner anymore. People were having a great time, it seemed, so Allie wasn't worried they would get up and leave if they knew Bill wasn't going to be at the party.

So why was she avoiding telling everyone? Was it to save face for herself?

Maybe she was just hoping that by saying it out loud so many times, it would make it true. This diner was Bill's family business—

it just didn't seem right that he wouldn't be there during the event—even if his friends in the kitchen were doing a great job. She wanted to show him the large framed piece she'd added on the wall by the booths. He had to show up at some point, right? He had to...

Allie barely had time to think, she was so busy refilling sodas, taking orders, handling the register, and greeting every single person who welcomed her to town.

"When's the live music happening?" a woman asked, one arm linked with her husband's. "We can't stay too late, but I don't want to miss that."

If Allie could just pull a lever and open a trap door so she could drop out of sight right at that moment, that would be perfect. Unfortunately, the renovations hadn't included that. She should have thought ahead and planned for making a fool of herself.

"Umm..." Allie started, looking at the woman, "Actually, I...I mean they...I couldn't—"

Zach Walker came up to the diner, put down a five-dollar bill, and interrupted her. "The live music is happenin' soon, so stick around," he said.

Allie glared at him, her eyes wide. Now what? She never did find anyone to play live music, and Zach knew that. So far, since it was still early, this couple had been the first who had asked her about it.

"Lookin' forward to it!" the woman said, and went back to the dance floor with her already-dancing husband, who probably was very pleased to have a date-night out tonight.

"What are you doing?" Allie asked Zach.

He grinned, his straight white teeth reflecting the sparkling lights across the long the back wall of the diner. He pushed the five toward her again, as if to remind her it was there.

"I think I need me some black coffee to make this work," he said. "Please."

She reached for coffee pot, keeping her eye on the handsome cowboy in front of her. "You better have a musician in your pocket, or you just got me into trouble."

Zach exhaled, as if he'd been holding his breath.

"I know," he said. "You don't have any live music."

Allie put her hand to her head, feeling the beginning of a stress headache come on. Bill had warned her she'd never find someone to play at the diner. She should have listened.

"I tried," she said. "I really tried. I thought for sure that *someone* would—Do you think people are going to feel like I'd led them on, just to get them in the door?"

"Not if you let me play my guitar," Zach said.

He didn't say it very loudly, so Allie had basically just read his lips. Was this for real? She hadn't even known that Zach played the guitar. Why hadn't Bill mentioned it? Maybe it was a brand-new thing and no one even knew about it yet.

"Are you...any good?" she asked.

"Well—"

"—nevermind. It doesn't matter if you're any good," Allie interrupted. "I shouldn't even have asked that. You're the only one who's even offered, and I definitely want you to play—if you're willing."

Zach smile widened. "Really?" he asked. "I knew you were lookin' for live music, but I didn't offer, 'cause... well, I've never played for anyone before, outside of campfire songs, an' I figured you'd want somebody more...special, for your special openin'."

"You're sweet," Allie said, laughing. "But I don't know whether to hug you, or kill you. Didn't you know how crazy I was going?" She poured his coffee and set it in front of him. "At this point I'd take somebody who told me they played the triangle."

Zach's smile faded. "Yeah, you're right. I should've said somethin', at least offered. Probably would've been better if I played for you so you could see what you're gettin' yourself into first."

"Well, that's comforting," she joked. "There's no time for that now. But everyone loves you here. And if you played around a campfire, well… that's good enough for me. I think you'll be great," she added, to pump him up. In reality, this was kind of a gamble.

On the bright side, no one would boo their own favorite cowboy off the stage, right? Hopefully.

Zach stood and nodded. "I'll run back to the ranch and grab my guitar. Shoulda brought it—I had a feelin' I'd need it tonight."

Allie handed him back his five-dollar bill. "And I'll have another hot coffee ready and waiting for you when you get back." As Zach turned to leave, Allie called after him "Oh hey—what type of music do you play?"

"Country songs," he said, as if that were the most obvious answer in the world. "What else?"

Zach Walker was a good man. He'd make some lucky woman a very happy wife… if he ever found that lucky woman.

Allie spent the next half-hour handing out food, (though with much less finesse than if she hadn't broken her thumb).

"Whaddja do to yourself, there?" a young man in a beat-up baseball hat asked, nodding toward her casted hand.

"The car airbag broke it," she said, for the millionth time to the millionth person (okay, not literally, but it felt like it).

Still, she answered him brightly. It was nice that folks around here even cared about what happened to a woman they'd just met. "I'm from Miami, so I still need to learn how to drive in snow!"

"Wow, that's somethin'," he said with a low whistle. He paused. "Bet you gave Big Bad Bill a heart attack."

Yes. Yes, she pretty much had. But the party was spinning around her, and there was no time to stop and think about everything that had happened, everything that had led to not having her partner by her side.

Bill, please please come.

An older gentleman came up to the diner. "I'd like a water with lemon," the man said jovially, "but hold the lemon."

Allie raised her eyebrows. "So just water? On ice?"

"Yes ma'am." He smiled, and pointed to a pleasant-looking middle-aged woman, chatting exuberantly at a booth with her friends. "My wife is especially excited you're doing bingo nights. We haven't had bingo since the church stopped doing it."

He tried to hand her cash, but Allie just gave him the glass without accepting payment, waving him off.

"No need, it's just tap water."

"'Well, thank you kindly, then." He leaned in so she could hear him better, or maybe because he didn't want others to hear. "You'll get plenty a' business here, 'specially if you can keep the prices fair—no one likes drivin' all the way to town just to catch a bite at a chain restaurant."

"That's what I'm hoping for," she admitted. "And that's a good tip. Good food for a good price, fair and square. I should ask Bill to add that to our sign."

"Where *is* Bill anyway?" he asked the guy next to him.

Please, Bill, where are you? Don't miss this.

Allie felt her eyes tear up, but she shook her head to clear her thoughts. She was only getting emotional because of all the excitement of the evening. She was doing fine without Bill—the grand opening was definitely a success. People were even using the dance floor, especially every time she put on a slower song, giving the couples who didn't usually have an opportunity to go out dancing in the mountains a chance to have some fun.

The front door burst open, letting another blast of frigid air into the warm diner. Zach Walker held up his guitar case and gave Allie a thumbs-up.

She came out from behind the counter to greet him with the promised extra mug of black coffee. "You are a lifesaver."

"Let's do this now," Zach said, and slurped his coffee, handing her the mug, "'fore I lose my nerve."

"You got it."

Allie made her way across the dance floor, saying hi to people as she went. It took her about five times longer to cross the room than it would have if it had been empty, but, hey, that's what a party was all about.

She stepped up onto this the wooden platform stage, and flipped the switch on the microphone stand she had purchased on eBay just for this purpose. Yup, that was how sure she had been that she would find live music.

And look at this… it had worked out after all. If only things with Bill would work out, too.

But some things were too big, too unrealistic, to hope for.

Stop it. There was no point in thinking about that. She already *did* know how things would turn out—it was her own stupid fault for falling in love with someone who couldn't fall in love back.

Allie spoke into the mic. "Let's see if this thing is working!"

She put extra cheer into her voice to cover for her previous thoughts. The mic worked as well as it had when she had first tested it a few days ago, and Allie looked over at Eric, Chris, and Jay, who gave her a thumbs-up.

"Thank you, everyone, for coming tonight to the Grand Opening of Uncle Freddy's Diner, named after, of course, our predecessor Fred Edwards."

They clapped, respect for their old friend.

"I'm so grateful that you all came, and for the kindness you've shown me as a new person in town," Allie continued.

Everyone was listening to her. Her mouth went dry, her throat suddenly parched. Butterflies fluttered around in her stomach as she took in the crowd.

Her gaze lifted to behind the counter, but Bill wasn't there, of course.

I can do this on my own— God help me.

"Keep an eye out for flyers," she said, "we're gonna have line dancing, and a whole lot of fun ... girls' night, bingo nights, some senior afternoon coffee days—and of course on the weekends, the big game will be on our screens. And half-price pitchers of soda pop."

Everyone clapped at this, and Allie beamed at them, her stage fright diminishing as quickly as it had come on. This was exactly what she had pictured, in all her best fantasies of how this would go, having a diner in the small town. A group of loyal customers who were genuinely excited to have her as part of the community.

"Let the boy play!" Ginger heckled with a laugh.

Allie hoped her face wasn't pink. "Yes! You all know Zach Walker, born and raised here in Bear Creek Saddle, and a real hard worker over at Melody Ranch." Allie paused.

It was almost like she was picking up on a bit of their accent, though she wasn't trying to. "He's got a little surprise for all of us… Turns out this handsome cowboy can also play guitar and sing!"

She waved Zach up to the stage. He was beet-red, and smiling in an adorable, bashful way that was completely incongruous with his six foot plus, masculine build.

He wouldn't offer to play if he was going to embarrass himself, right? Maybe. Zach Walker was the kind of guy who might, just so she'd be able to keep her word to the people in town about the live music.

She handed Zach the mic and stepped down. *Fingers crossed.*

"Well," he said in his deep baritone. "Miss Allie says I can sing an' play guitar, but she's just goin' on faith."

Everyone laughed, and Allie could see both the people in the crowd and Zach loosening up noticeably before her very eyes.

"Let's start with some old favorites," Zach said, and he went right into a Johnny Cash song.

Whoa.

His voice wasn't just good—it was great. This guy, with his movie-star good looks and incredible talent—he should be a country music star in his own right. What was he doing throwing hay on a ranch in the mountains of Idaho?

A low voice spoke in her ear, and Allie jumped.

She whirled around. "Bill!"

Relief flooded through her, relief mixed with joy all at once. He came. Bill was here for her.

She wanted to hug him, but she didn't dare. "I'm so glad you made it."

"I'm glad I made it too," he said, and she followed him to behind the counter, where they could talk without interrupting the music. "I've been texting with the boys in the kitchen, checkin' up on everything. It was kinda hard for me to come tonight."

He looked from the stage to Allie in surprise, as if just noticing that his ranch hand was rocking the house.

"How on earth did you get Zach to sing in public?" he asked.

Allie shrugged her shoulders. "I think he took pity on me, because he actually offered himself."

"He's not into attention," Bill murmured. "I'm impressed he's up there at all."

"Why do you suppose he's still living here, instead of going off to Nashville or something?" Allie asked. "No offense to you and the ranch, of course."

"Nah," Bill said, giving her a look as if he couldn't imagine why anyone would want to go to a city and be famous. "Some folks like the simple life. Zach's one of 'em. Me too."

"Me too," she added.

"No need to share yourself with the whole world," he said, nodding.

This was the longest conversation they'd had without one of them getting upset in…a while.

"Yeah," Allie said. "Sometimes, I guess a place like Bear Creek Saddle could become your whole world. I love it here. I wouldn't want to leave either." She looked up into Bill's eyes. "I don't ever want to leave."

What she didn't say, what she *couldn't* say, was that she never wanted to leave because this was where Bill was. And wherever he was, Allie wanted to be, too.

Bill looked around. "We need to talk. Privately," he said, his face serious.

Oh no.

What was going to happen? Tonight had been going so well. She didn't want to hear Bill tell her—yet again—how he didn't want anything to do with her or the diner. How he was still planning on packing up and heading for his hunting cabin up north.

She wanted to pretend, just for one night, that he wasn't leaving her. That he wasn't leaving to go live alone...without her.

"I didn't mean to lay it on so thick," Allie said hurriedly. "I just meant that I would never want to leave here personally. I wasn't making a jab about you leaving to live off the grid. I get it."

"I still need to talk with you. It's too loud in here. We could either step outside, or we could go up to your apartment."

Allie nodded. "It's freezing outside," she said, staring out the window into the dark night. "You haven't seen how I've decorated the apartment. It's really looking like home now."

"Just remember, that was your call," Bill said. "I'm not just tryin' to get you upstairs."

Allie frowned at him, but then she saw Bill's smirk.

"Ha ha," she said.

She took his hand in hers to lead him upstairs. But as soon as their hands touched, she dropped hold of him quickly. His touch ignited something in her. Could he feel it too?

Bill followed Allie toward the back of the diner. He stopped suddenly and pointed to a framed portrait on the wall by the booths.

"This is new," Bill said.

She couldn't tell from his voice if it was good new, or bad new. The portrait on the wall was a picture of his Uncle Fred. The town library, it turned out, had been a treasure trove of local newspaper clippings. It was when Fred Edwards had been a younger man, and had his diner showcased in the paper for being part of a pie eating contest.

The pictures showed him, along with the article, framed. An engraved plaque below it said: *Freddy's Diner was originally owned and operated by our own "Big Bad Bill" Edwards' beloved uncle, Fred Edwards. Fred ran a great diner, and he is missed. Rest in peace.*

Below that, Allie had listed the date of Fred's birth and the date of his death.

Bill reached toward the wall, and touched the frame. "That's real nice," he said, his voice thick with emotion. "I like that."

He swallowed hard, and Allie could see he was holding back tears. Her poor cowboy… So much loss, in such a short time. She knew he'd loved his uncle very much. It made it even more wonderful of him that he'd accepted the changes Allie wanted to make to his uncle's diner without too much of a fight. Bill was a good guy. A really good guy.

"I'm glad you like it," Allie said softly.

She unlocked the door to the stairway that went upstairs, and Bill followed, locking the door behind them so no one would follow them.

"Wow," Bill said, "this place looks great."

Allie smiled, and gave him a quick tour. Very quick, considering how small the apartment was.

"It's amazing what a woman's touch can do," he said. "You've really made this place a home."

"I had no choice," Allie said. She had no bitterness in her voice, only sadness. "It's not really a home," she said. "Not until —"

Not until you're in it with me.

But she couldn't say that. That's why she had to stop herself before she went too far, before she said too much. Begging Bill to be with her wasn't the answer. He knew how she felt. There was no reason for her to lose her dignity, as well as lose her chance at love.

Bill pulled her into his arms, her face pressed against his muscular chest, the scent of him filling her with an overwhelming desire to never let go.

"I'm not moving to my hunting cabin," he said. "And the guys an' I have already talked about them buyin' the ranch."

Allie looked up at his face, barely daring to believe it was true. "What did they say to you? Zach didn't mention anything about it."

"They're buying the ranch," Bill said. "It's profitable, and the money that it brings in will pay for itself. Now the guys can be the ranch-owners they were meant to be."

Allie smiled. "That's exciting. Congratulations…to all of you."

"They're renaming the place to Bear Creek Saddle Ranch. Can't say I blame 'em."

Hmm. The new name was simple and perfect. Just right for a ranch run by a crew of hardworking, bachelor cowboys. Much better than the name Melody Ranch, in that respect.

"So are you going to just stay on there?" Allie asked. "I mean… your house is there. Where are you going to live?"

"I'll be stayin' on there, until I find a place more suiting to my…current stage in life."

"What stage in life are you in?" Allie laughed. "You're too

young for a midlife crisis, mister. Don't go out and buy a sports car or something."

"I like my truck just fine." Bill smiled, his gray eyes like the sky after the storm. "I'm in… I'm in this stage where I'm not bogged down in the past. Is that a stage? In the present?"

Bill laughed, and Allie joined him.

"That's a good stage to be in," she said.

What did this mean, though—for *them*? "If you're not living in the past anymore," she said, "does that mean…"

No. She couldn't bring herself to ask him. Bill had to be the one who pursued her, or she would never know if he ever would have pursued her on his own, or if she had just talked him into being with her.

I'm here. Falling for you. Catch me, please catch me…

"Allie," Bill said, "I want to be with you. Even though it's scary. Even though I'm afraid to lose you. I was afraid to fall in love with you…"

He paused, and the word *love* seemed to float in the air between them. Had he meant to say it?

"It doesn't matter that I was afraid to fall in love with you," Bill continued. "Because it's already happened—whether I want it to have happened or not."

Allie didn't know what to think, or what to say.

"Whether you want to or not," she repeated. "I know you didn't want to fall… in love with me. But if it's happening anyway…is it okay? Are you…okay?"

Bill looked down at her, holding her against him. "I'd feel a lot better 'bout it, if I knew that you had feelings for me too. You don't need to love me, not yet. I know it's fast." He dropped his head so his forehead touched hers. They were so close. "But if I just knew there was a chance…"

A thick wet tear rolled down Allie's cheek. A tear of happiness. "I already love you."

He wiped the tear from her cheek. "Say that again," he said softly.

"I love you, Bill."

"I love you, Allie," he whispered.

His lips met her own, pressing against her with all the intensity and emotion that flowed between them like electricity. The deep, raw wounds from the past healed as their souls' connection pulled them closer together.

This kiss, their first kiss after declaring their love for one another… Allie would never forget this moment. She would taste his lips on hers for the rest of eternity.

Her cell phone buzzed with a text from Eric—a photo of the standing ovation for their own Zach Walker down below.

Bill looked over at her phone and smiled. "We can't let this go to that boy's head," he said, and laughed.

Allie had almost forgotten that the grand opening was going on downstairs—nothing was as important as this moment, here with Bill. But she'd been dreaming about the opening of her diner for a long time, and she knew that with Bill there, everything—all of her dreams—would come to fruition.

Thank you, God.

She wanted to experience that, too.

"Let's go downstairs," Allie said. "There're a lot of people who are going to want to hear you say something about the diner, maybe about Fred."

Bill smiled and kissed her again. "I think I can handle that," he said. "But as soon as the party's over, we have a lot of time to make up for."

Downstairs, people were in full swing, dancing to Zach's music. Eric and Chris had taken over for her behind the counter, filling orders with more exuberance than skill. No one seemed to mind.

Allie flashed them a thumbs-up sign as she came downstairs, hand-in-hand with Bill. The guys must've seen the open affection between her and Bill—they gave her a thumbs-up sign right back.

When Zach finished his set, Bill stepped up onto the small stage and took the mic. Everyone cheered.

"Woot!" a girl in the back yelled with enthusiasm. "Big Bad Bill! Big Bad Bill!"

Allie laughed and even joined in as the crowd chanted his nickname and cheered.

Bill motioned with his hands for the crowd to simmer down. "I know my uncle Freddy woulda been real proud of what Allie Crawford has done here. And he'd have been proud of all of us, for comin' together again in his favorite place in the world. Right here, in Uncle Freddy's Diner."

Everyone cheered. Allie couldn't help but notice some of the older men in the back patting each other on the back, like they were consoling each other, and there for each other. Uncle Freddy's close friends.

"I have some changes to announce," Bill said. "You're gonna see me here at this diner, quite a lot. No, not eatin'—"

"Yeah, right," someone heckled good-naturedly.

"Well, maybe a little eating," he said, "and just doin' whatever jobs my Allie here may need me to do. The boys in back seem to have the kitchen in fine order. As for the ranch—"

Zach and the guys started hollering before the words were even out of Bill's mouth.

"As for Bear Creek Saddle Ranch—that's the name now, folks, don't forget it—I'm proud to introduce my boys, my friends—our very own ranchers Zach Walker, Eric Hunt, Chris Green, and Jay Thomas, as the new owners."

The guys all stood up and clapped each other on the back, tipping their hats to the cheering girls, huge smiles brightening their handsome faces as they took in the thunderous applause.

"You all know they've been runnin' the ranch for a while now," Bill said with a laugh. "I'm just glad to make it official."

"You there—with the smile," Ginger called from the crowd, gesturing toward Bill, "who are you, and what did you do with Big Bad Bill?"

Everybody laughed, shouts of "Yeah!" and even one "Good to have the real Bill back!" sounded all at once in a joyous outburst.

Bill smiled at Allie, and put his hand down to lift her up onto the stage next to him.

"Seems like God put this woman right here for a reason." His voice dropped, practically a whisper that only she could here. "I think Jesus used you to bring me back to life," he said. "I really do."

Thank you, Jesus. Tears formed in her eyes at his raw honesty.

He cleared his throat and spoke up louder, so everyone could here. "An' I intend to keep her around."

Bill dropped to one knee.

Allie gasped. "What are you doing?"

"Askin' you to marry me." He took his Stetson off and set it on his knee. "If you want to. Ain't got no ring yet."

"Yes," she said, so softly that only he could hear her. "Yes!" she said louder, and the crowd cheered.

Right there in front of everyone in their diner, Bill swooped Allie into his arms, and kissed her.

The End

Acknowledgements

FIRST AND FOREMOST, I would like to give the glory to God for making me a storyteller, for which I am forever grateful! Thank you for sending us your Son.

Thank you to my readers. Without you, I would be writing into the abyss. And a special shoutout goes to the Shoshanna Street Team—thank you for your support, and for spreading the word!

Thank you to those who helped me with the original edition of this story, written as *I Am Not Your Melody* by Shoshanna Evers, especially Annette Stone and Heather Thurmeier. Thank you to the Christian inspirational authors who have encouraged me to write this book the way I really wanted to write it, and for my readers for joining me on this journey with my new name as Shoshanna Gabriel, and my new genre. I'm thrilled that the Bear Creek Saddle books will still be published.

Thank you to my new agent, Karen Solem of SpencerHill Associates, for your support.

Thank you to my beta-readers, and an extra-special thank you to Bonnie Paulson.

Thank you to my cover artist, Rob Sturtz, from SelfPubBookCovers.com for my cover. I co-founded SelfPubBookCovers.com with Rob to help fulfill my dream of having quality covers at an affordable price available to all indie authors, instantly. If you're a writer, too, you might want to check out the amazing artists we have on board!

Last on the list but not in my heart: thank you, Dear Husband, for being awesome and for being my soulmate, and to my children, for going to bed so sweetly every night, so Mommy can write while the household sleeps. I love you!

About Shoshanna Gabriel

SHOSHANNA GABRIEL WAS previously known as Shoshanna Evers, a *New York Times* and *USA Today* bestselling author who wrote over twenty-plus secular romance novels and novellas, and published with big New York publishers, small presses, and through indie-publishing. After much thought and prayer, she decided to **change her life and career path to be for God's glory**. Shoshanna Gabriel is currently working on writing Christian inspirational romance novels. For a detailed explanation of this big change, read her blog post "Saying Goodbye to Erotic Romance" (http://bit.ly/GoodbyeErotica).

While published as Shoshanna Evers, Amazon had listed her as one of the "Most Popular Authors in Romance," as well as one of the "Most Popular Authors in Contemporary Romance". Reviewers have said Shoshanna has "…**beautiful writing**, and a **truly imaginative** and wonderfully descriptive storyline" (Night Owl Reviews) with stories where "the plot is fresh and the pacing excellent, **the emotions…real and poignant**." (The Romance Studio). She hopes to bring her gift of storytelling to her new inspirational books written under the Gabriel name.

Shoshanna used to work as a syndicated advice columnist in NY and a registered nurse, but now she's a full-time author and a home-schooling mom of three. She is also **the co-founder of SelfPubBookCovers.com**, the world's largest selection of high quality, affordable book covers for indie authors, available instantly. She lives with her family and three big dogs in Northern Idaho, and loves to connect with readers on social media.

*Faithfully Ever Afters…*ShoshannaGabriel.com

Want to know when my next book comes out?

Sign up for my newsletter to hear about new releases first, and read excerpts you won't find in the sample pages!
ShoshannaGabriel.com/subscribe

Visit ShoshannaGabriel.com/contests for monthly giveaways of different inspirational romance novels!

Let's be BFF's!

@ShoshnnaGabriel (Twitter.com/ShoshnnaGabriel)
@ShoshannaEvers (Twitter.com/ShoshannaEvers)
Facebook (facebook.com/ShoshannaGabriel)

To my readers:

If you enjoyed this book, I'd love if you could **leave an honest review**! Reviews are so important; thank you for taking the time—I really appreciate it!

Bonus Content!

HERE'S A SNEAK PREVIEW OF *BEAR CREEK SADDLE COWBOY*, BOOK 2 IN THE BEAR CREEK SADDLE SERIES.

First, an overview:

Bear Creek Saddle Cowboy: Book 2 in the Bear Creek Saddle Series

A YOUNG WOMAN ESCAPES an abusive relationship in NYC, determined to find her independence in the beautiful mountains of north Idaho…until a handsome rancher reaches out to her, and she finds herself questioning everything she thought she knew about relationships and faith.

When Megan Moore leaves New York City to live in the country — far away from the crowds, the traffic, and a controlling ex-fiancé — she finds herself way over her head in the mountains of rural northern Idaho.

Zach Walker runs a cattle ranch with his friends in small-town Bear Creek Saddle. It's not every day a beautiful woman falls into his life — and he's been looking for a wife. He just had no idea the exact opposite of the traditional-type cowgirl he thought he wanted would end up needing his help. What's a red-blooded man to do when he can't get his mind off the wrong woman?

As for Megan, she can't let her growing friendship with the handsome, guitar-strumming cowboy put her at risk for getting into a smothering relationship again. She came to Bear Creek Saddle to prove to herself she could make it on her own—certainly without any help from a rancher. But Zach's solid faith inspires Megan as she works to change her life.

Megan doesn't know anything about country life, so if she's going to make it on her own in Idaho, she'll need to learn fast. Zach is willing to show her the ropes.

Especially when he realizes Megan just might be the wife he's looking for, after all—and that sometimes, God puts a man and a woman into each other's lives for a reason...

KEEP READING FOR THE FIRST CHAPTER OF ZACH
AND MEGAN'S STORY...

Bear Creek Saddle Cowboy

BOOK 2 IN THE BEAR CREEK SADDLE SERIES
BY SHOSHANNA GABRIEL

BEGINNING OF BOOK 2

"Look at the birds of the air; they do not sow or reap or store away in barns, and yet your heavenly Father feeds them. Are you not much more valuable than they? Can any one of you by worrying add a single hour to your life?" *Matthew 6:26-27*

ALMOST THERE.

Megan Moore pulled into the gas station about ten miles or so outside of her final destination, according to the GPS. The place was deserted.

She stepped out and stretched with abandon—it felt good to move around after being in the car for so long. A week of driving cross-country from New York to northern Idaho made her muscles knotty and tight. Around her, the cooler summer evening air was still warm enough to leave her jacket draped across the passenger seat while she pumped the gas.

With her hand on the pump and her back to her twenty-year old two-door blue Eclipse, Megan scanned her surroundings. She was accustomed to being constantly presented with a new potential danger to evaluate. But there weren't any people around, and not even many places to hide behind if someone were lying in wait. Everywhere, evergreen-covered mountains towered in the near distance, separated from her by wide expanses of fields.

So different from Manhattan—exactly what she'd been hoping for. There had only been a few vehicles on the road during what would have been rush-hour on the East Coast.

One of those vehicles was coming her way now.

Who's this? The keychain dangling from her pocket tapped reassuringly against her thigh, the small canister of pepper spray her back-up plan if the driver of the truck wasn't friendly. Or was too friendly.

A beat-up red pick-up truck pulled up to the other side of the pump. There was a split second of no sound but the rumble of its engine, then *WOOF WOOF WOOF!*

Megan startled when the big black dog barked at her from inside the truck.

"Don't mind her," a young man said as one long, muscular, denim-clad leg climbed out of the truck, followed by the rest of the perfect specimen of Idaho cowboy.

Megan wasn't sure if he was talking to her, or to the dog, since his handsome face was partially in shadow from the light-colored cowboy hat on his head. A Stetson? That was the only kind of hat she knew the name of. Light stubble covered the strong lines of his jaw. The unkempt brown tendrils kissing the back of his neck could've benefitted from a comb, but this man didn't look like the type to play with his hair.

His striking good looks were so distracting she almost forgot why he was talking to her in the first place. If he was even talking to her at all, that is.

"Wh-what?" Megan asked, setting the pump back in its holder.

She should go—get in her car and leave now that she was done pumping gas. But instead, she wanted to stay. Stay to just...look at him. Heat flushed her face... and she probably wouldn't be able to blame that on the mild weather.

He nodded toward his black lab. "That's jus' Inky. Everyone knows Inky—she's tamer than I am."

"Oh, that's good," Megan said. "Wait...are *you* tame?"

The man looked at her in surprise at the question, as if noticing for the first time that she was a woman alone, fidgeting with her keys.

"Almost always," he said. "Neither of us bite, anyhow."

He grinned at her, flashing his nice white teeth for a moment as he picked up the windshield sponge and got to work cleaning the dead bugs off the truck's front grille.

"That's good," she repeated, and peered over into his truck at the dog again in an attempt to not stare at its owner.

"New York, huh?" the cowboy asked her over his shoulder.

"What gave me away?" Maybe he could tell by her accent. Her clothes? The fact that she physically jumped a bit when his big dog barked?

He turned to face her, and her attention drifted to his warm, kind eyes. Green with flecks of brown.

"Your license plate," he said, interrupting her thoughts. "New York.... Bit of a culture shock for ya here."

Megan smiled and shook her head. "Well, maybe, but it's a *welcome* culture shock, if that makes sense."

"Sure does." He set the windshield cleaner back in its bucket of murky water and wiped his hands on his jeans. "And here I was thinkin' you must've gotten pretty lost to end up all the way out here. Middle of nowhere."

Megan smiled at the unexpected pleasure of having a person to talk with, after days of only the radio to listen to.

"I traveled through some mountainy stretches of nowhere to get here," she said. "It's not really nowhere if there's a gas station." For a moment, Megan let herself fall into his gaze, enveloped by the cowboy's handsome green eyes.

"That's a fact," he agreed, his lip curling up in a half-smile of amusement.

His arm, draped over the side of the pump, made him look casual and friendly. As if he were enjoying chatting with her.

Stop. The last thing she needed was to have her thoughts dominated by a man's charms.

"Well, at least I'm not lost," she said, a nervous laugh escaping her throat. The only time Megan had really felt lost was when she was still in New York, trying to work up the guts to make the big move.

Driving here was the easy part.

The familiar safety of her car called to her, and she slid into the driver's seat. "So. Um...see you later."

"You betcha." He tipped his hat in a lazy way that indicated how customary the gesture was to him.

She smiled out her window in response and lifted her hand in what she hoped was a properly friendly 'bye-neighbor' wave instead of an 'I'm-from-NY-where-we-don't-wave' wave.

The dog barked at her again, but Megan didn't mind. *That's just Inky.* Now she was one of the 'everyone' who knew Inky, too. And maybe she *would* see that cowboy later. It was a small town, after all.

Wow. Megan shook the silly grin off her face so she could focus on driving back out onto the road without crashing into something.

If he was representative of the type of man who inhabited her soon-to-be new hometown, she wouldn't be as uneasy here as she was around men in New York. All of her ex's colleagues had the same too-slick feel that Todd did—as if their skilled small talk and unnoticed-by-most grabby glances at her were part of a carefully built façade—one that would crumble should she ever stand up for herself, or stray from the herd.

Not so with this cowboy. He felt…genuine. As on edge as Megan had been beneath the friendly chit-chat, he still somehow gave off the vibe that he would sooner protect her from danger than *be* the danger. Megan couldn't know that for sure, of course. Their chance encounter had lasted all of about three minutes. It was just her gut-instinct talking. But weren't gut instincts pretty much always right? If only she'd listened to it sooner with Todd…

How crazy was it that humans were the only animal that ignored their instinctual silent alarm bells ringing? If a gazelle did that, if it saw the lion approach but didn't run because it didn't want to make a scene, or look stupid, or be wrong about the lion…well, fortunately for gazelles, they were smarter than she was in that regard.

But who said 'you betcha' without irony, anymore, anyhow? Megan grinned out at the road ahead of her, her grip relaxing on the steering wheel a bit. The deeper into Idaho she got, the more different it seemed from New York. Like cutting pieces off of a tart apple and finding a hearty potato underneath. That different.

She was close, so very close to Bear Creek Saddle. Her new home.

And she already had made an acquaintance. Sort of…she didn't even know You-Betcha-Man's name. Or if he lived in town or was just passing through. She should've asked him. Maybe he would've even asked her out, to show her around.

No. Stop.

If she was never going to tie herself down to a man again, then why should she even care who the friendly cowboy with green eyes really was?

And yet she did care. *You betcha.*

* * *

That night, Megan leaned down and gently blew into the struggling fire. "Come, on," she urged the flames softly. "You can do it."

Considering this was her first-ever campfire, it was going much better than she'd dared to hope. *She* was doing better, even. If someone had told Megan even a few months ago that she would find herself sitting in the woods in the mountains of northern Idaho—single—she wouldn't have believed them.

The idea of leaving Todd, leaving New York City and her unexciting part-time job in human resources had occurred to her, of course. That wouldn't have been the shocker that would have kept her from believing this would happen. There were more than a few moments when his cloying manipulation left her feeling suffocated, times she stared out the window at work and felt jealous of the construction workers laughing and yelling to each other across the street. But if she could go back in time and tell herself that she would actually get the guts to *do* it, to leave him for real and not just in her daydreams—to run off into a brand-new life… there was no way she'd have believed it. Not even if it were future-Megan telling her.

So all that considered, struggling flames aside, she was doing all right. More than all right.

The forest itself was an adventure—the breeze flowing through the evergreen trees and the way the wildflowers popped up throughout the clearing excited her senses in a way that city lights never had.

Megan hadn't seen this much nature in all of her twenty-three years stuck in New York. She'd gotten out before it was too late, at least, before she ended up miserably married. This was the last place anyone (*Todd*) would think to look for her, camping alone in the middle of nowhere, as You-Betcha-Man had called it.

The beautiful, awesome, thank-goodness-it's-not-the-city, nowhere. Not even a gas station in sight.

"I think it's time," she murmured.

She didn't have to rummage in her bag too long to find the three-dollar bottle of sparkling cider she'd gotten from the store that sold her the firewood. They'd sold wine, too, but if she was going to start fresh then she'd be better off letting go of her vices. Thus the non-alcoholic bubbly.

The twist-off cap dampened the ceremonial "pop" sound, but it still launched her into celebration-mode.

"To a fresh start," she told the fire, lifting the bottle. She took a sip straight from it, since she hadn't planned ahead enough to bring a glass.

The sky was filled with stars, bright pinpoints bedazzling the wide expanse above her. It had (presumably) *always* been filled with stars—but in New York City, there were too many lights to ever see them. Stars may as well have never existed for her.

But now they did.

Underneath the tight control Todd held over her, surely Megan had always been there, buried beneath his good intentions gone wrong just as the stars were too overpowered by the city lights to shine.

She may as well have never existed, either. But now, she did. Now Megan had a chance to shine as well.

"I'll drink to that," she murmured, and took a sip. The taste reminded her of celebrating New Year's Eve with her sister when she was twelve. For three dollars, it could've been worse.

There was a feeling of independence that camping out in the woods imparted. It was a new feeling. On the long drive from New York to northern Idaho, cross-country practically, she hadn't made use of her brand-new tent once. Instead, she'd stopped at cheap motels along the way, watching their boxy TV sets and eating their free continental breakfasts in the morning. It'd been too scary to risk camping for the very first time while on the road.

But Megan wasn't on the road anymore…not now that she'd

arrived at Bear Creek Saddle. This small town in the mountains of northern Idaho would be her new home.

Megan laughed and shook her head. Before she'd checked Google Maps, she'd been under the murky impression—despite having a college education—that Idaho was somewhere in the middle of America, like Iowa. Whoops.

Kinda embarrassing when she realized she'd been conflating Iowa and Idaho her whole life (the few times she'd had reason to think of states that started with the letter *I*, that is), but even more so when she found out none of her Manhattan colleagues even knew where Idaho was either. It was like, who cared about any place that wasn't New York or Los Angeles?

"I do," she said, unaware she murmured to herself out loud.

As she'd discovered after a few map clicks, Bear Creek Saddle was a tiny dot right near the top of America, the best-kept secret in the Pacific Northwest. Idaho shared a border with Canada, with the skinny panhandle of northern Idaho sandwiched between Washington and Montana. The photograph she'd seen online while searching for somewhere (anywhere that was nowhere) had called to her, enticing her to click on the picture of this little town, and study every bit of it. Such a great mental escape from all the concrete in the city.

It was that one photo—with its incredible mountain peaks, lakes, and evergreen trees—that hooked her. It had been captioned with the location of the town, so here she was.

The whole state of Idaho was sparsely populated—NYC alone had *way* more people. The few who lived in north Idaho appeared to be hardy and self-sufficient, the exact opposite of how she viewed herself.

You-Betcha-Man was probably like that, too. There was something incredibly appealing about a man who knew his way around just about everything. She could just picture him, with that smile he'd flashed her, building a...barn or something...whatever men in Idaho did. He'd know exactly what needed to be done, whereas she had no idea where to even start.

Stop. Megan sighed and pushed the thought of him from her mind. Another man was the last thing she needed right now. If she felt like going the relationship route again, she'd be better off shackling her feet together instead. The end result would be the same. Stumbling on her path to freedom.

A breeze blew over her, and the flames tilted perilously. In her jacket, she was quite comfy, despite the little chill that had crept into the air. Thank goodness she'd decided to run away from it all in the summertime. Northern Idaho was probably not the best place to visit for the first time in winter.

When her pot of Chef Boyardee was ready to be pulled off the flames, she poured the chunky pasta into her metal camping bowl, and dug in with the metal spork that had come with it.

"Mmmm." *This is the life.*

Before, it had been a lifetime of waking up to a buzzing alarm, and heading out the door every single day—first to Pace University on the NYC campus up until a year ago, then to work in a low-level, part-time position in HR that her Bachelors degree should be wiping its feet on. After being told what to do and where to go and how to behave, the mere thought of living here in this little rural mountain town, collecting eggs from squawking chickens, milking a cow...doing whatever else it was that homesteaders did (make hay?)...well, the fantasy calmed her.

She could have her own little house; she'd make friends with the people who lived here. Not with You-Betcha-Man though, because he made her too…*interested* to just be friends with.

Getting *interested* was dangerous. She knew that much.

Time would go by, she imagined, and perhaps they'd start calling her a spinster. Megan liked the idea of that. Spinsters weren't tied to a man, spinsters took care of themselves, and then got called spinsters for having the guts to not want to be dependent on *any* man.

"Call me what you want," she murmured to the townsfolk in her imagination—those who might call her a spinster when they saw how far she stayed away from a wedding chapel. Ha! Or was she thinking of Regency England times?

She took another sip of the sparkling cider.

Thank goodness Todd had asked her to marry him—because the *wrongness* of it had hit her like ice-water, and that was what woke her up. If she didn't want to be stuck in the same anxiety-ridden rut forever, she'd had to get away—before it was too late. Living with Todd had been so bad from day one. Surely God had a hand in that. It helped her to wake up to the fact that her life needed to completely change.

If she didn't have such a stubborn independent streak—and a growing distaste for city life—Todd could have been her Prince Charming. Who wouldn't love having a man swoop in and pay for everything and take care of everything… and control everything… and obsess over all the little ways she wasn't doing things exactly the way he wanted her to… yeah.

Every day Megan had spent in Manhattan had the effect of sensitizing her a little more. Each stranger who bumped into her on the street added insult to injury, every siren that howled past her, jangled her nerves just a little bit more.

Maybe it was city life that was killing her. Maybe it was being under Todd's thumb. Or the soul-sucking treadmill of going to a job she hated to make money that paid for a lifestyle she'd never asked for.

Tomorrow, when the sun was up again, she'd find a dumpster somewhere to get rid of her trash. It wasn't littering if she put it all in a garbage bag with every intention of throwing it out, right? Were there even dumpsters in the mountains? Or was that just in all the dark back-alleys in New York? Fun times, back-alleys, where she got to walk with her pepper-spray in hand, her head on a swivel, just waiting to get mugged or worse. No, that wasn't utopia to her, not anymore.

Megan took another cleansing breath of night air to clear her thoughts.

If she'd been looking for the exact opposite of New York, then northern Idaho was it. This town encompassed so much land, huge mountains and lakes—but it only had a population of 649. That meant there was a lot of land for each person. A lot of space to find herself.

Bear Creek Saddle was going to have to change their sign to say POPULATION: 650 …because Megan was staying. This would be home now.

She tilted her head back, letting her long, dark hair fall out of her face, and searched the sky. Beyond the tall trees, diamonds sparkled down at her from above.

Here she would start fresh, and be independent, and *Be. Happy*. No matter what it took, no matter what she had to do to make it happen. They could even call her Ol' Spinster Megan (she sort of hoped that nickname took).

In fact, she was starting to feel better already.

* * *

The sun was barely over the horizon when Zach Walker parked his red pickup truck where the dirt road ran out. He'd go on foot from here. His lips pursed to whistle, when he stopped himself. He was just so used to having Inky with him, but she was sitting this walk out to let a crack on her back paw heal a bit. Poor ol' girl.

Zach walked along the long, twisty trail, a trail beaten-down by his feet more than anything else. He'd been taking this route all summer, basically since the last of the snow melted on the mountain. If he wanted to bag an elk when the season started in September, he had to scout out his hunting grounds first.

There were plenty of men who'd just hunt wherever they could drive to, hike out for a few minutes, open up a six pack, and wait it out. Privately, Zach thought hunters like that wasted their hard-won elk tags. But those men weren't really his competition. His friends at the ranch were all looking to fill their freezers as well, and they were good at it. Maybe they should team up to help each other.

Zach preferred going *au natural*—hunting with a bow and arrow. He'd been an archer since he was a kid. There was something about the feel of it; the bow was an extension of his body when he pulled that string back, his hand coming right up to his cheek, and letting that arrow fly. The gun on his hip was for protection, but not for hunting.

His phone buzzed in his back pocket, alerting him to a text.

It was Paige again. Her text read: *"Good morning, sunshine! Want company for scouting? I'm wide awake!"*

Of course. Who else would want to go scouting for elk at dawn when they didn't even hunt? She was a sweetheart, but every time he texted with her, or let her in for coffee when she stopped by the ranch, he felt like he was just leading her on. They'd broken up almost five years ago, officially—after being together all through high school and for a few years after—but she and his mother were still planning on Zach coming around, and settling down with Paige.

It wasn't going to happen.

Not because Paige wasn't a great girl, but because he wasn't in love with her. She deserved to be with a man who loved her properly. And he deserved to be with a woman he was crazy in love with, too. He would do everything in his power to ensure his future marriage was nothing like his own parents' had been.

"Thanks anyway," he texted back. *"I'm already out."*

Zach sniffed the air. Was that... Chef Boyardee? He shook his head. That didn't make any sense. He was in the middle of the woods, in the mountains. But as he had been walking up, he'd only smelled the crisp air, the grass and dirt beneath his feet, and sometimes, the sweet scent of wildflowers blooming along the trail. The evergreen trees had a smell too, that fresh piney scent that was better than any air freshener could ever hope to replicate.

Paige interrupted his train of thought with another text, a frowny face, followed by: *"Don't forget about the Bill & Allie's harvest party! Let me know, we'll have so much FUN!! ;)"*

He slid his phone back into his pocket. Yeah, parties were fun—and Zach could eat with the best of 'em—but the "Sadie

Hawkins" thing where only the girls were asking out the guys had put him on the spot. Wonder how many guys had chewed out Bill and Allie for putting out those stupid flyers, to celebrate their new deep fryer. Free french fries for every couple. *Couple* being the key word—probably Allie's way of ensuring twice as many people would show up. She was business-smart like that. Crazy thing was, the place was going to be *packed.*

Telling Paige he was too busy to go with her hadn't worked, because she'd just made sure his schedule was cleared (that mainly involved talking to his mom). Now the only way to avoid leading her on even more was by telling her the painful truth—yes, he supposed he could go to the party, but he didn't think it was a good idea to go together. Man. That conversation was going to be uncomfortable for them both. Maybe he could just give her money for french fries and send her on her way without him. *Nah.*

It wasn't that he didn't want to settle down. He definitely did—just not with Paige. There came a time in a man's life when he had to get serious about finding a wife, raising a family. Now that the ranch was on firm ground, he had no more excuses. He was ready for it.

What Zach really wanted, when he thought about it, was a kid. A kid he could be a real father to, someone so different from how his own father was to him. Someone who wouldn't leave his kid, ever. First step to creating a loving family was for Zach to find a wife.

All he wanted was a woman he was madly in love with, who also happened to be a cowgirl who could help him run the ranch, cook up a storm, be well-liked in town and in church, be great with kids, and of course, want to marry him too. And beautiful, if at all possible. Not too much to ask, or maybe it was.

Paige fit the bill completely—except he wasn't in love with her, not even a bit. He'd already tried to fall in love with her exactly because she was so perfect, but there are some things that can't be forced. Love is one of them.

Working the ranch didn't exactly provide too many chances to meet a woman he didn't already know. He'd dated some of the girls from town in the past few years. Zach was starting to think the only way to find a wife would be to leave the ranch and travel some, or start internet dating. Man.

The slightest scent of canned pasta carried to him on a slow breeze. What on earth? His woods weren't the same as they were yesterday morning. Something was different.

Zach deviated off the trail, checking his whereabouts carefully, and followed his nose. He wasn't more than a few hundred yards from the trail when he spotted what had to be the messiest campsite he'd ever seen.

A brand-new tent, clearly never used before, was set up, still zipped up tight. Despite the fact that the sun had been up for over an hour, he had a feeling that the owner of the tent was inside, sleeping in. A long-dead fire had left its ashes in what he could only suppose was meant to be a crude fire pit.

Sitting right out on the rocks around the charred logs was a used dish. Next to that, a tipped-over glass bottle of what had probably been white wine or champagne, judging by the tiny puddle in the dirt around the mouth of the bottle. But that was just a drop in the bucket compared to the worst of it—a ripped open trash bag, the contents spread around the campsite like confetti.

"Everyone had themselves a party," he grumbled.

Some sort of animal must have gotten into the trash bag that was on the ground, tied up and held down by a stone. They had torn it open, littering the campsite with granola bar wrappers, baby wipes, juice boxes, chewing gum, tissues, and yes… two cans of Chef Boyardee, open. Something must've scared them off, because Zach could still smell the pasta that reminded him of visiting with his friend when he was a kid.

If he could smell the campsite from yards away, the bears would be able to catch the scent a lot farther off. And the wolves. It was nice of the camper to try not to litter, but obviously this person was a moron. Who else invites bears to their campground like that? They may as well send out invitations.

Something pink and white caught his eye. A lady's socks? Yes. Hanging from a tree branch behind the tent, as if the socks had been washed and left out to dry.

New-York-Girl.

It had to be. The campsite wasn't from a crew of out-of-town teens partying, after all. He hadn't seen the girl's little blue car, but it was probably around here somewhere. What had she been thinking?

For some reason, Zach felt almost…betrayed. He'd hadn't thought she was the sort to get drunk by herself and pass out in the tent. She must be hurting more than he'd picked up on. He'd seen this before, but only with a couple of homeless guys traveling through.

It's not like he actually knew her, just because he'd spoken a few words with her at the gas station the day before, anyway. And yeah, she'd set up camp practically in his own backyard, but that didn't mean much. It wasn't hard to do considering how much land the Bear Creek Saddle Ranch covered on the edge of town.

The girl was lucky nothing worse had happened during the night, with hungry animals prowling around, looking for free food.

Why hadn't the sun woken her up?

Zach walked right up to the tent and tried to peer inside. All he could see was a bundle of sleeping bag and some of her beautiful dark hair poking out. Was she even breathing? He watched closely until he saw the sleeping bag move slightly.

All right, she wasn't dead. Good. He forced himself to look away. It wasn't…appropriate to watch a woman sleep. She was too vulnerable like this. He should forget scouting and pull up a log, sit watch until she came to.

Should he?

It wasn't his business anyway. It only *felt* like his business because he'd mentally claimed this area as "his" hunting spot, and, if he was honest with himself, because he had really liked her when they'd met. There was a longing inside of her that drew him in.

And she's beautiful. Right. But that didn't matter. Her beauty and one chance meeting didn't make her his personal responsibility.

In Idaho, people took care of themselves. It was one thing to be neighborly, and give a helping hand. It was another to try and police folks.

No one else was likely to come up this way past her tent. She was safe where she was.

Let her do her thing. It wasn't his life, it was hers to live how she

chose to. Zach backed out of New-York-Girl's campsite and
returned to his hike. He'd check in on her on his way back, just to
make sure she was still alive. She was kinda petite to have drunk
that whole bottle of…whatever it was.

Zach was about a quarter-mile up the trail, the part where it
wound down closer to the creek. It soothed his senses to hear the
running water as it bubbled over the rocks, past the fallen
branches, leaving little white peaks in the water—visible
disruptions of the water's motion. He sat on the ground, resting
on his elbows, and took a load off his feet.

This was the best. He loved his morning walks in the woods.
Even though he lived spitting distance from all his friends, he was
glad none of them joined him in the morning. They each had their
own routines. It was nice to have this solitude, sometimes.

Zach closed his eyes, and listened to the water. A vision of the
willowy girl from New York smiling shyly up at him flitted behind
his closed lid, and he grinned to himself.

Are you tame, she'd asked him… His first instinct had been to
joke in response, but the look of resigned fear in the girl's eyes
had made him slow down and tell her the truth—she had nothing
to fear from him. Or Inky, with her ouchie on her big gray paw
pad, poor dog.

The branches rustled down on the other side of the creek.
Something was amiss. He sat up, alert, and stared at the area the
sound came from.

Zach had leaned up against a fallen log, the same hollow tree
he'd used as a backrest for the past two years. Something was
different this time, though.

A small patch of brown fur clung to the bark. It looked like an animal had rubbed itself against the log, scratching its back, perhaps? Or maybe even just passing by it. He picked it off and rubbed the fur between his fingers. Bear fur.

Uh oh.

Zach stood up slowly, and looked around the grass for tracks. Sure enough he saw some stomped down grass, but more importantly… a big pile of bear scat. Wasn't too old, either, from the looks of it. How could he have missed this?

"HEY bear," he said loudly, to warn the animal he was in the area, and to stay clear. "HEY bear."

Bears in his part of northern Idaho were brown bears more often than not (much more dangerous than the black bears, which weren't exactly friendly themselves), and he didn't want to risk meeting this one face-to-face. He had to get back to the truck, and come back the next day—equipped with bear spray as a just-in-case—and hopefully the bear would have moved on.

What about the girl, passed out in her tent?

"Oh no." He shook his head. *Not good.*

If there were a bear in this immediate area, she was in danger, and didn't even know it. If Inky had been there, she would have sniffed out that bear early on and possibly even frightened it off with barking.

Zach searched the area with his eyes, ears, and nose, looking for any sign of the bear. He could kick himself for being so distracted before that he'd forgotten what he was supposed to be doing—scouting. Looking for tracks and droppings. If he'd been doing that after he'd left the campsite instead of worrying about New-York-Girl, he would have noticed signs of the bear long before he got close enough to hear something…big…moving through the bushes.

The more he looked, the more signs he saw…but no actual bear. *Where is it?*

Then—a large, dark shape moved slowly behind the trees, then disappeared again. Yup. That was a bear all right. First one he'd seen in years this close up that hadn't been dead, stuffed and on a stand.

"I'm not dancing with a bear today, my friend," he whispered.

He put his arms up, to appear even larger, and walked backwards out of the area, keeping his eye on the trees where he'd seen the bear, until he was back on the trail.

Hikers were supposed to make noise to warn bears off, but at that moment his instinct told him to stay quiet and unnoticed. He rushed back down the trail, his eyes and ears wide open so he wouldn't accidentally sneak up on the bear—or any of its cubs, if it was a mama bear, which would make it even more defensive—and ran back toward the campsite.

This time, he was going to wake that woman up.

* * *

Megan lay in her tent, and snuggled into her sleeping bag. Celebrating her independence last night had been exciting—when it wasn't terrifying. She'd stayed up way too late, her mind racing with possibilities for her future. All the things she could do with her life, and all the things she could no longer do, if she was going to try and live right.

Her water bottle called to her, and she gulped some down to rehydrate.

Her first night trying to sleep in the woods hadn't been so bad at all. A little scary at times, maybe. The forest was alive with sound at night, from the crickets chirping to the flapping of wings above the trees. Somewhere in the far-off distance, a train whistle blew, her only reminder that civilization was just a car ride away.

She pulled her phone out of her purse, and checked the time. 6:30 AM, and battery at 5%.

Ugh. That was way too early. Why did she have to wake up at the same time her alarm had always woken her? She'd thrown that stupid thing in the trash, and now for vengeance it was haunting her internal body clock. But, she wouldn't mind getting the fire going. That way she could heat up some water for coffee.

Getting a fire going… a lot of work for a little hot water. Ha. Maybe she should've stayed in a motel after all?

No—that was sleepy-Megan-think. This was her home now. And if there's no hotel in town, then camping was the way to go.

It was what she wanted, anyway, right? To live off the land. It was going to be hard enough going from living in New York City to living self-sufficiently in northern Idaho, without adding never-even-been-camping-before to her list of reasons why she shouldn't be doing this.

The sound of something moving outside the tent caught her attention. *What is that?*

Then—a voice. A man's voice.

"Hey there," the man called, with just a touch of country twang to it—

(like You-Betcha's voice)

—the sound deeply melodic while terrifying…simply by the fact that she could hear it at all.

No one else was supposed to be here. How had this man found her? What did he want?

"Hate to wake you up, ma'am, but you need to come on out now."

Oh my goodness. Oh my goodness oh my goodness…

Her heart raced. She'd thought she had escaped the dangers of predatorial men when she'd left the subways and the dark alleys of New York City behind. Now she was alone in the woods, with no one around for miles—except for this man. A man who wanted her to come out of the tent.

No way.

"Ma'am, you okay in there?" the man called, an edge to his voice now. "You need to wake up right now and uh…get a move on—" he interrupted himself. "Can you hear me, ma'am?"

She held her breath, terrified. How did he know she was even inside the tent? She could have left her campsite to go hiking, for all he knew. She didn't answer him.

Just go away.

"I'm comin' in to check on you, ma'am."

Oh no. He was going to come in if she didn't come out? *No.* She would not be bullied by another man. This was *her new life*, it had to be different. Jerks like her ex didn't belong here. Her heart continued to race, but her thoughts remained clear.

Time to use that adrenaline. Fight or flight, right? *How about both?*

Megan grabbed her keychain, and readied her pastel purple cylinder of pepper spray. She gripped it tightly in her hand. If she had to use it, she'd have to hold her breath and turn her face away when she sprayed, so she wouldn't get any of it in her own eyes.

She'd never actually used the thing before. Hopefully it would work.

Please God protect me.

A shadow at the front of the tent darkened the inside where she crouched. The man outside the tent was on his knees just a few feet away from her—separated only by a thin layer of material. The opening unzipped slowly before her eyes, from the bottom up, the action as mesmerizing as it was dangerous.

Light drifted in past the opening from the outside. She could see dusty jeans, as the man kneeled on the ground and opened her tent.

Megan wanted to scream—instead, fear paralyzed her and only a choked whimper escaped her throat. Who would hear her, anyway? The pepper spray was her protection, not some unlikely rescue. It probably only took about three seconds for the man to get that zipper all the way up, but it felt like a movie playing in slow-motion before her eyes.

A sturdy-looking young man with a familiar cowboy hat ducked his head inside, and stared at her—*it was him*! The cowboy! His grass-green eyes widened with surprise, his lips slightly open, as if he'd forgotten to exhale. The stubble on his jaw, darker than the tousle of brown hair falling onto his forehead from under his hat, glinted in the rising sun.

"Oh, you're awak—" he started to say.

"You *followed* me," she gasped, not having enough air in her lungs to scream the words the way she wanted to.

How could her gut instinct have been so wrong? Why was the gas-station cowboy here, uninvited, in her tent? He was supposed to be one of the good ones!

Or maybe there was a tattoo on her forehead that said VICTIM. Men who wanted to hurt her could see it clear as day.

Men like her ex, men like the cowboy she'd been so sure had been different. How had he found her?

Don't mess this up.

Megan aimed the pepper spray right at his handsome (*no! Terrifying!*) face. "GET OUT."

When he didn't immediately move, she pushed the trigger down.

The cowboy turned his head instantly, but OH NO where was the spray? Nothing came out of the cylinder!

"Whoa," he shouted—as if she were a panicked horse—and put his hands up in defense. "Whoa there!"

"Stupid pepper spray not working I will HIT you, you scary mountain man rapist cowboy what on EARTH are you doing in my tent?!"

The words flew out of her mouth at a high-speed rate, all running together in her terror, which admittedly, sounded a lot more like furious anger when she expressed it.

With a desperate howl, Megan wrapped her fingers around the pepper spray instead and slammed her fist into his nose. She'd never hit anyone before, and GOODNESS GRACIOUS it hurt her hand, even with the cylinder taking the brunt of it for her.

The man grunted in a way that sounded as if he were trying to keep from roaring like a lion. Holding it in, holding back. He was quick—he grabbed her wrist on its way down, not letting her get another blow in.

"Let go of me—" she shrieked.

"—stop hitting me!" he yelled. With a quick movement, he threw her own hand back at her and jumped up, standing once again outside her tent.

Blood dripped from his nose, and the man dropped his face into his hand, as if to make sure it was still attached. Why hadn't the pepper spray worked?

"You hit me good," the man said, and pulled his shirt up to wipe the blood away, revealing a muscular abdomen she was too frightened to appreciate.

It was important to notice, though, for the sake of the sketch artist—if she made it out of the mountains. Was this why he hadn't introduced himself at the gas station?

That one punch was her fight, but now what—flight? Could she run all the way to her car in time, before You-Betcha started chasing her? All he had to do to get her now was to lunge…and he'd be back inside her tent, on top of her. And then what?

If all she'd done was anger this guy, what would he do in retaliation?

"Get away," she said. "Go away from my tent." Her voice was high and shaky to her ears. She sounded like someone she didn't even know.

"LEAVE ME ALONE!" That sounded more like she meant it. Oh man.

The cowboy put his hands up again, as if to show her he was no threat. The nosebleed had stopped. "I didn't mean to scare you. It's me! From the gas station. I'm not…seriously, I'm not gonna hurt you."

I can run. I can do it. She just needed to get out of the tent. The door to which this stranger—that's what he really was—now blocked with his imposing physique.

"There's a bear in the area," the man said, gesturing behind him, toward the creek. "We gotta get outta here. That's what I came here to tell you."

A bear? The word filtered through her mind as a potential threat, but she had zero experience with bears. If there really even were a bear, was that more of an immediate danger than a man who had apparently stalked her?

"Move away NOW," she said. "I need to get out of my tent. STEP AWAY."

The keys, now weapons between her fingers, were hot in her hand. They had been cold only a few moments earlier, when she first picked them up to spray the cowboy. He wouldn't want a punch from her spiked fist now, that was for sure.

"Why did you break into my tent?" she demanded, crouched inside, peering out the opening at him—as if the thin material would save her from this man, as if it were a house of bricks instead of less-than-straw.

"Why'd ya hit me?" he growled. He paused, as if realizing her question answered his own. "You remember me, right?" He sighed. "I didn't follow you or…nothin' like that."

"Of course I remember you." Her cheeks burned. "This is a *bit of a coincidence*, isn't it?" she asked, managing some sarcasm despite her fear. "How'd you find me, then?"

"You found *me*, New-York-Girl. You're campin' right behind my land, on my stompin' grounds."

What? How had that happened? She hadn't even known for sure he lived in Bear Creek Saddle, much less where his land was. The look of confusion on her face must've shown through, because You-Betcha-Man smirked.

"It's all right," he said, his lower lip crooked in the half-smile. "I ain't mad 'bout that."

Megan took a breath. *He* wasn't mad at *her?* Please.

"Camp where you want, lady. But we should get outta here." He stilled, cocking his head to listen for…something.

A bear…?

"Explain why you thought you could break into my tent uninvited," she said through gritted teeth.

"We got no time for that—"

"Well," she said, "then I'm not moving."

He sighed. "I'd been hollerin' for you to come out," he said. "I saw your empty bottle—you were passed out drunk."

"I was *sleeping*," she spat. "Not passed out. And I'm not drunk."

"Well, you sure showed me." He tentatively touched the bridge of his nose and glared in her direction from under the rim of his hat. "Don't worry, you didn't break it."

Ha. Like she was worried that she'd injured him. Megan was more concerned about the fact that her one weapon, the pepper spray, had completely failed her in her time of need.

"Go away then," she said, brandishing her key-loaded fist at him.

"I won't hit a girl, but I will keep you from hitting *me*, you understand?"

"Don't you touch me. I will poke your eyes out with my keys if I have to." The steel in her voice matched her resolve.

"You keep threatenin' me, ma'am," he said, taking a long stride backward, "Next time I'm gonna throw your keys so far into the woods the bear'll find 'em 'fore you do."

"You will not," she gasped, pulling her spiky fist closer to her chest. But he was big, and he looked serious.

"You're settin' there arguing when there's a bear nearby and you've got the messiest camp I've ever seen."

Mess?! He was a liar. He was trying to lure her out again so he could serial-kill her.

"I didn't leave a mess," she said indignantly. "I put everything away in the trash bag. You're lying." *For what purpose?*

"I make it a point to not tell lies," he said, as if he were offended. Was he? "I smelled your food when I was walkin' up the trail," he added. "And if I can smell it—"

"Why can't you just leave?" she interrupted.

She sniffed the air, and yeah, maybe there was the tiniest whiff of pasta sauce. But if there really was a bear, would it really want pasta?

"There is a bear *nearby*, in this area. A big, *brown* bear," he said, emphasizing the word *brown* like it should mean something to her. "It will find its way to your camp just by followin' its nose. Just like I did. Now stop arguin' and come outta that tent 'fore I go in there."

"I don't see a bear." She crossed her arms protectively across her chest. "But I will hit you again if you come in here."

The man shook his head, his lips tight. "And I'll take you out kickin' and screamin' if I think it'll save you from getting mauled."

Then she noticed the gun, holstered on the man's right hip. *A gun.* He was armed. She'd never seen anyone with a gun before, other than a cop, or in the movies. Was it on him at the gas station, and she just hadn't noticed it under his shirt?

"Okay, okay," she said softly, putting her hands up. "Just don't shoot me."

"What the...? I'm not gonna shoot you—what is wrong with

you, lady? We don't have time for chit-chat!"

Megan kept her hands in the air, and nodded toward his side-arm.

The cowboy scoffed, as if she'd offended him. "These are the mountains. There's wildlife. This is…come on, this is *Idaho*."

This man was clearly a danger. Or was he? The hairs on the back of her neck should be standing up on end right now, the way they used to when Todd would get going on something. Every bit of logic she had told her to keep away from both a stranger *and* a hypothetical bear, but instinctually, she wanted to have that man stand next to her, somehow. Maybe even slightly in front of her, in case the bear got in their path.

"I get why you reacted that way to me," he said, tentatively touching his nose, wincing. "Why you punched me. No hard feelings—and you don't need to look at me like that. I ain't gonna hurt you. But we need to go. Now."

"Why should I believe that?" she asked. "Or believe that I'm camping practically in your backyard. You could even be making up the bear."

The words were barely out of her mouth when she heard…something. A growl. Not even quite a growl, but definitely a bear sound. Or a…monster. It didn't sound too close, or was it? *Stop.*

"Wh-what was that?" she whispered.

"Well," he said, not whispering. "That sure does sound like the bear I made up, don't it? Told you it was comin' this way. Last I saw it was down at the creek, and that ain't more than a mile east."

With his accent, he pronounced "creek" like "crick." She liked the sound of it. Just not the context.

Okay, this bear was probably no longer hypothetical.

"How close is the bear now?" she whispered. "I heard that growl."

"No need to be scared," he said, as if he sensed her fear might paralyze her. He was so large and strong, the role of protector seemed to come naturally to him. "Sounds carry pretty far in the woods, all right? You can hear a bird singin' from miles away. It's closer than that, but it won't come near us, not right now."

He reached his hand out to her, to help her get out of the tent. The cowboy seemed impossibly tall, towering over her. Megan looked up at him, her eyes wide.

What am I going to do?

Another sound—this one louder. Rustling in the bushes, another growl of something big.

"That sounded close," she whispered.

"You're safe with me," he urged. "That bear won't wanna tangle with me. It can smell and hear us—it doesn't wanna die, either."

Go with the man she'd just hit? *Or risk meeting the bear?*

"Now," he ordered, his voice deep and powerful.

With the keys still in her hand, she pushed out of her tent, purposefully ignoring the stranger's big hand, proffered to her.

Immediately, he took hold of her hand anyway, as if afraid she'd run in the wrong direction. Panic tightened the breath in her throat until she looked up at his face, and saw no menace there. There was a look of concern in his (*beautiful*) green eyes, and she let the strength of his grip comfort her for a moment, her breath normalizing. It was if he really wanted to help her, and didn't even care that she'd punched him in the face only a moment before.

His skin against hers tingled with awareness where their palms met.

"Come with me," he said.

She was used to being ordered around, yet it still bred resentment. It felt a bit different with You-Betcha-Man, perhaps because he truly had her best interests at heart, instead of just wanting to dominate her. Maybe.

No. She was useless at determining whether a man was good or not. Hadn't she proven that to herself again and again? It didn't matter if there was something about his commanding tone she respected (or even liked).

Megan pulled her hand out from his. Somehow she had gone from being alone and independent for the first time in her life, to having a man ordering her around again, in short order.

She hadn't even made it on her own a full twenty-four hours.

"Hey," the man said, and gestured with his head for her to keep up. "If the bear hears us, he'll stay away. Bears don't wanna mess with people. But they *do* want food. I bet your campsite smells pretty good to the animals right now."

She glanced back through the trees at the mess, scanning the bushes to find the source of the growling. The trash bag she'd thought would keep her campsite clean had been torn to bits, and food wrappers, her leftovers, and empty cans of pasta and meat were strewn everywhere.

"Fine," she said. "I don't want to meet a bear either."

They moved briskly, walking through the zigzagging trail, passing trees, wildflowers, and beautiful scenery that—in another situation—she'd have stopped to admire. Everything here was

Instagram-worthy. Not like that mattered anymore. She'd had to delete all of her social media accounts to keep her ex from contacting her.

At a sharp turn in the trail, the cowboy put his heavy hand on her shoulder. She startled under his touch.

"Please don't," she whispered, even though his hand on her felt…comforting, almost. He was (*kind, but still*) a stranger and she didn't know what he was up to.

"I told you I'm not gonna hurt you," he said, but he kept his large, warm hand firmly on her shoulder. "Don't want you to break an ankle, is all."

"Okay."

Was it okay, though? Megan tried to compare the nervous, butterfly feeling she had right now, the feeling that made her tremble when this stranger touched her or spoke to her, to the sick feeling of dread she'd get when Todd did the same.

It was different. This man was not her ex, or at least, he wasn't tripping the same alarms. Even if he was telling her what to do and sort of…manhandling her.

"Okay," she repeated softly.

It seemed as if he could walk this trail blind, as if he'd followed it so many times he knew it by feel alone.

"Where are we going?" she asked, needing two steps to keep up with just one of his long strides. His hand on her body forced her to move faster, to stay with him. "Where can we go that's safe from a bear?"

"Well, we're puttin' distance between us, and we're also headed toward my pickup truck. We get to the truck, and drive, and then we're fine." He gestured for her to keep up. "The bear will almost for sure go into your campsite, so we need to let her do that, and then go back tomorrow for your stuff after she's moved on."

"Oh! I left everything in there. I need my phone," Megan said. "And my purse. My ID! I have to go back and get them." The rest of her cash was in that purse too.

"Not happening."

The cowboy kept walking, and his hand on her shoulder had gone from comforting to constraining in that moment. Her muscles tensed.

"I won't start my new life in Idaho as a charity case," she said, her voice as firm as his had been. "If there's any chance I might lose the only possessions I took with me, then I have to go back."

Would she even be able to access her mother's inheritance without proof of identity in a new town? Megan looked back at the path behind them, toward the campsite.

"Not on my watch," he said.

He dropped his hand from her shoulder to the back of her upper arm, as if quietly preparing to hold her against her will if she made a break for it. There was no pressure in the touch, but Megan knew from his superior size and muscle mass that he could grip her and pull her away from danger in an instant if he felt he needed to.

Yet the flutters in her stomach weren't from fear. Something about this man excited her senses, made her ultra-aware of his every movement, every point of contact between his body and her own.

"I told you I'd keep you safe," he said, his voice hushed and gravelly. "You need the help."

"I need my purse. And I'm going back." She shoved his hand off her, and he let it fall.

From the strength of him, she knew he wouldn't have let go if he hadn't agreed to. Megan gripped her keys in her fist. If he tried to stop her, would she fight him, again? Even knowing he would undoubtedly win?

With a quick movement, he grabbed the keys from her fist. "I warned ya."

"Hey!" she gasped. "Wait—please don't throw them into the woods. I need my car keys."

He paused. "Fair 'nough."

Megan grumbled under her breath in response. He kept on walking—this time without his hand on her for guidance—jingling her keys. She followed him, even though the thought of being stranded without any money, identification, or communication was almost as scary as the threat of a bear. More so, since she hadn't ever really thought about what it meant to have a bear hanging out nearby.

"Ma'am, I can tell you're new here, and you don't get it. That's a brown bear that's makin' its way toward the campsite you want to go to. They're bigger and meaner than black bears, all right? I saw it with my own two eyes."

"But I haven't," she said. Now that they were away from the camp, uncertainty blurred the edges of the situation. What if those growling sounds were a product of fear and her imagination, and not a bear at all? "You're a stranger—and you could be...*tricking* me to go with you, for all I know."

"This is Bear Creek Saddle," he drawled. *Baayer Crick Saddle*, sounded like. "It wasn't named that for no good reason."

Touché.

"A person'd have to be from Mars to not know this is bear country," he continued. "And I hate to break it to ya, but *I'm* not the stranger here. You are." He grinned at her. "Maybe I should be scared of you. You do pack a mean punch."

"Ha ha," she deadpanned.

"Just sayin', now's probably not the best time to be acting all cynical," he advised.

"Where I'm from—"

"—Mars?" he suggested.

"New York," she said, ignoring his jab. "And in New York, that's not being cynical, it's called being safe."

Without another word, Megan turned on her heel and ran as fast as she could along the twisty trail, trying her best to make sure she didn't go off the trail at the wrong spot.

This wasn't a suicide mission, right? The rustling they'd heard hadn't actually been in the campsite, it was farther out in the woods. Same with the growl. Sounds carried a long way in the woods, isn't that what the cowboy had told her? So she had time to get her stuff.

She had no choice but to get her phone, ID, and money. Other than a duffel bag of clothing, her backpack and her purse, she'd left most of her belongings in New York. This was important—without her own things, her own money, how could she be independent at all?

Did she want him to follow her back to the campsite? Yes. Wait—no. That would be scary. If he chased her....

There was no way she'd be able to outrun him. With his long, athletic strides, he'd catch up to her no matter what. And then what would happen, once he had her?

Megan gave her head a little shake. Back to reality. He wasn't chasing her. If he had been, she'd already be caught. Strangely, the thought didn't frighten her. He seemed like the sort of guy she could count on, even if she didn't even know his name.

Stop. All this unwarranted attraction was just the product of high stress, endorphins and hormones flying everywhere. Was it unwarranted, though? Goodness, the man dripped testosterone with every move he made, every word from his lips. She couldn't blame herself for being attracted to a cowboy on a mission.

As long as that mission didn't interfere with hers.

She veered off the trail to get to the clearing, approaching cautiously.

The campsite was still a mess, but there was no bear. Was it in the shadows, waiting to pounce? *No, thank God.* Even if the bear were only a short distance away, at least it wasn't there.

She ran past the trash and ducked into the tent. Megan put on the backpack she'd been using as an overnight bag, and grabbed her little purse and cell phone.

Did she have time to take down the tent? *No. No way.* It had taken her almost half an hour to put it up for the first time, and she'd never broken down a tent before. But where would she stay, without it?

Branches broke somewhere out there. A loud cracking noise. She jumped, and a nearby bird took flight. Better to get in her car. She hefted her backpack and stepped out of the tent, leaving the campsite as quickly as possible.

Please don't let me run into the bear. Keep the bear far, far away.

The cowboy met her at the trail, his eyes flashing, his

posture… intimidating. As if the big bad cowboy couldn't believe she'd put herself (and him) in danger for something as superficial as a cell phone and a purse.

At least now she could be one hundred percent sure he hadn't been trying to trick her all along. That meant his intentions might even be as good as he said they were. As good as she'd hoped they were.

"Next time you run off, I ain't followin' to save you, pretty girl or not," he said, shaking his head. "We're headin' the wrong way. You don't want to head *toward* a bear. Someone told me that once."

Did he just say she was a pretty girl?

"I didn't make you follow," she said. "I told you what *I* was going to do. You can do whatever you want."

She pushed past him, her hand connecting with rock-hard muscle. He didn't budge—it was like pushing against a mountain. Still, she ran ahead, glancing back to see where he was.

Megan gasped as the man took one big stride, falling briskly in line with her.

"Hey—you don't need to be scared of me." His voice softened. "I'm on your side, okay?"

"Why? You don't even know me. And I punched you in the nose."

"This is my neck of the woods, and you're in it," he said, ticking the points off on his callused fingers. "I can't blame you for defendin' yourself. That, and you don't have a clue what your doin' out here."

The way he said it, as if it were simple fact, and nothing against her personally, took the sting out of the words. Brown hair peeked out from under his hat in the back, some strands falling against his forehead.

"I do so know what I'm doing," she said. "Sort of."

For now, though, she'd walk with him. She'd rather have this big cowboy with a gun next to her if that bear found its way to their path, than try to make a go of it on her own.

"You really did a number on me," he said. He didn't sound angry though, for some reason.

"Good. I just wish the pepper spray had worked. My hand still hurts from punching you."

"Yeah," he muttered, and handed the keychain back to her. "You coulda punched me with the keys." He nodded, as if thinking it through. "Yup. Next time, if a man enters your tent, you poke him in the eyes with the keys straight away. Don't just threaten or he'll take 'em from you, like I did before."

Megan raised her eyebrows at him.

"You didn't know I was one a' the good guys," he explained. "You're lucky. I could've been—"

"Todd..." she whispered, her voice cracking a bit.

"I was gonna say 'someone with bad intentions,'" he finished.

"Is your nose okay?" She reached up to his face, suddenly feeling the urge to fix what she'd done to the man who may have saved her from getting mauled. "It doesn't look too bad. I'm glad I didn't blind you. That would have been awful."

"But if I was goin' to hurt you instead of try to help you, you'd have my full permission—not that you need it—to defend yourself. Welcome to Idaho."

Ha. Welcome to Idaho. Yeah. She hid her smile by lowering her head.

Finally, they arrived at her car. *Hallelujah.* It felt like seeing home after being away. She slid into the drivers' seat with a sigh of relief (*safe!*), and looked up at him through the window.

But he was already opening the passenger door. "I need to hitch a ride. My pickup's just down a ways."

He had to fold his long, muscular body practically in half to fit into her old two door Nissan Eclipse.

"Just a ride, okay?" she asked. The last thing she wanted to do was lead him on, make him think she kind of liked him (even if it was true). Megan couldn't handle being hurt by a man again…and she knew nothing about this man who had broken into her tent and was now attached to her hip. "Nothing else."

"Ma'am," he said, staring straight down into her eyes. "We need to set something straight, you an' I."

Megan swallowed hard, and started the engine, anything to not look at him.

"We started on the wrong foot," he said, "'cause ya thought I'd followed you. That I was breakin' into your tent to hurt you. I'm a 'scary mountain man rapist cowboy,' right?"

"I'm sorry," she apologized, not knowing why she needed to, just that maybe it would stop the conversation.

"Don't need to be sorry. But I'm pretty sure I heard you scream that right before you punched me in the face." He frowned, as if her words had hurt him more than the punch. "That's not me. That's just what you're afraid I am. But you're wrong."

The words "I'm sorry" almost escaped her lips again, but instead she put the car in drive and gave it some gas.

The car wouldn't drive.

"You've got to be kidding me," she groaned.

"All right," the cowboy said, as if he wasn't surprised a bit. "If her engine starts but she won't drive…" he paused, and furrowed his brow in concentration. "Could be your transmission, or the CV joint. I can check 'er out and see what's wrong," he offered, "if you want. For now, we're safe in the car, anyways."

"That's good," she said. "Being safe is good."

She tapped her fingers on the steering wheel, trying not to stare at the handsome cowboy in her passenger seat, and revved the engine again.

"Don't flood the engine," he said.

"Don't tell me what to do," she shot back, with more force than she intended.

"Your car, your rules." He took his big tan hat off, and set it in his lap.

His brown hair was deliciously tousled. He looked like he would've been a blond child. Even the stubble on his jaw had some blond hairs scattered through the brown ones…

Focus. She turned the key in the ignition again and tried to drive. Nada.

She paused to let her agitation seep out of her voice before she spoke. "You said you have your pickup truck somewhere?"

"Sure do. We'll have to hoof it." He set his hat back on his head, as if ready to jump out of the car that second.

"Wait! What about the bear?"

"We're practically on the main road," he said. "I don't think the bear's comin' down this way. I think she was just waitin' for us to leave your campsite so she could roam around there. She'd rather snack than mess with us. We should be fine to walk."

Megan breathed a sigh of relief, and they got out of her car. She touched the hood forlornly. What a pity, to leave her baby alone in the woods.

"Do you need a moment?" he asked, and grinned. His straight white teeth gleamed in the sunlight.

Wow… so shiny.

She gazed at his smile, momentarily awestruck, before reality set back in. "Hey… can I get a ride with you, please?"

"My truck, my rules," he said. "Got it?"

"Fine," she muttered.

"I wouldn't just leave you alone out here, anyway," he said, putting his hat back on. "What kinda man do you think I am?"

"I don't know. I don't even know your name," she said. "Can we…start over? Pretend we just met again now, after the gas station?"

"Yes, ma'am," he said. "I appreciate that."

She stuck her hand out. "I'm Megan Moore; nice to meet you."

He tipped his hat and shook her hand. "Name's Zach Walker."

"Looks like someone bopped you one in the nose, huh?" she teased, giddy with the idea of starting over. "Bar fight?"

"Nah, just me bein' stupid. I'm lucky I didn't get myself shot. Frankly, I'm lucky to be alive."

Megan laughed. "Welcome to Idaho. Where not getting killed makes you a lucky guy."

They arrived at his pickup truck. It was a bit beat up and it had mud on the tires, but it was a ride.

Zach reached his arm out like he was going to grasp her

shoulder, and she took a step back, stumbling a bit over a stone. But no—he was just reaching for the passenger door.

Huh. He was opening the door for her. How…chivalrous. When was the last time a man had done that for her?

A small, quiet voice inside her whispered: *he's a good guy—it's okay.*

She tamped down the thought. *Don't get comfortable.* She didn't need a man to open the door. That was the whole point of coming out here alone—to do things on her own, including opening doors. She could probably handle that much, at least.

She paused before stepping up into the truck. If her sister could see her now, Lindsay would be yelling at her for getting into a stranger's truck.

"I think I know the answer to this," she sighed, "but for my sister's sake, I have to ask, just to be sure: this isn't all an elaborate plan so you can murder me, right, Zach Walker?"

"Never killed a person before, don't plan on startin' now." He paused. "You don't have to believe me, New-York-Girl…Megan. Keep your fistful of keys handy. Maybe you'll let me teach you how to shoot one of these days, if you stick around."

Okay. That was promising.

Lord, I'm trusting You…please keep me safe.

She got in the truck.

Want to keep reading?

Search for my name, Shoshanna Gabriel,
at your favorite book retailer,
and find the rest of the Bear Creek Saddle Series!

Pick up a book and visit Bear Creek Saddle, Idaho, anytime—
you're always welcome HOME.

GOD BLESS!

♥Shoshanna Gabriel